Burning Stars
Gnoll Discovery

Burning Stars

Gnoll Discovery

Champagne Universe Series

Book 4

By A. K. Brown

Squid Publishing Edition License Notes

Copyright © 2019 A.K. Brown

All rights reserved.

ISBN-13 978-0-9945412-8-4

Prologue

The art of war teaches us to rely not on the likelihood of the enemy's attack not coming, but on our own readiness to repel him.

Sun Tzu – Art of War

The galaxy is a cold, feral place, where species live and die by hand and claw. The myriad of intelligent beings clash and jostle one another for the mere right to exist. Out of the ashes of war, the fabric of sentient society was wrought into a pyramidal class structure split by strength and technology. Older, more established species rule as Patrons over younger Client races that floundered at the base. Each race striving to find their way along the path toward the apex. New primitive species are pawns to be manipulated by the intrusive galactic community.

Below even the lowest of these interstellar players is a young fresh species with innocent eyes that jumped their way into the Galactic Collective. This singular naive race is shocked at the devastating consequences of failure... *Extinction.*

♦♦♦

Lizard Scout Ship, *Silent Claw*

The crew of the *Silent Claw* sat helplessly as they watched the battle for Earth unfold. Their stealth ship continued on a ballistic course through the Sol system, hidden from the Human sensors. What initially seemed like a decisive Lizard victory, had suddenly turned sour as the Human ships made impossible FTL jumps from within the gravity-well of their Sun. Somehow, they counteracted the gravity well's influence on their Alcubierre Drive(A-FTL) (Faster Than Light drive). It was thought impossible to enter subspace inside a gravity well of a star. The gravitational distortion would rip the ship apart. And yet, the Humans had found a way.

The most startling of the reports were from Fleet War Leader Darvus himself, they described Humans boarding their warships. How could they have done that? Why did the Humans think they should attempt it? Sane species don't board Lizard warships if they want to live, they run away as fast as they can.

After two months of sailing through the system undetected, the scout reached the limit of the Sun's gravity well.

"Prepare to return home to Draconus," the War-leader said as he stared at the latest scans of the system. Humans were still conducting SAR operations.

The scout ship *Silent Claw* dropped into subspace and took off back to the Empire to report the Humans' victory. The War Leader knew the Emperor will order these Humans eradicated, they were already too dangerous. The Emperor will also want their amazing subspace technology.

◆◆◆

Bridge, Gnoll Frigate, *Light Bringer*

The frigate spiraled around the enormous Gnoll freighter as it chased after the smaller, faster pirate ship. The bulky freighter with its spars jutting from the central spine hindered the Gnoll frigate's response to the pirate's evasive maneuvers. The pirate ship's rear laser struck out at the frigate's shields which erupted in bright green energy sparkles.

The main viewscreens on the bridge of the second escorting frigate briefly dimmed from the bright lightning-like energy discharges.

"Do not let it escape," Lord Volund's deep voice commanded. The bridge crew's reaction was immediate, the order sent shivers down the spine of the Ferret at the helm. The last Ferret helmsman had disappeared after a mere three months. The Gnoll Lord had a nasty habit of slaying the inefficient or sending them to the mines of Sar'grett; a dirty, sulfate-mining outpost deep within Gnoll territory.

"Take out their engines," he commanded the Tactical Officer.

The blue furred officer, with a scar that ran the length of his eye to the jaw, twitched his wet black snout before spinning his right-hand control to target and fire the frigate's heavy forward laser cannons.

The powerful Gnoll lasers struck near the pirate ship's dorsal fin. The smaller vessel flashed in a sphere of golden light as its shields flickered then failed. The ship flipped end on end, its main engines turned to slag. Plasma and atmosphere spewed out in great gouts as the ship tumbled before it smashed into the freighter's shielded comm hub. Plasma and radioactive plating blew away from the damaged outer hull of the freighter, forming a sphere of expanding radioactive debris.

The tactical officer onboard the *Light Bringer* nervously pawed his nose as he turned to Lord Volund, his furry body shaking with fear.

The feline stood, stretching his full eight feet, his dark mane cascaded down his back. "You fool!" he snarled as his eyes zeroed in on the culprit.

The scar-faced ferret cringed, huddling low as he could to the console.

"Incoming message from the *Wild Roar*, my lord," interrupted the blue-green comms officer, breaking the tension.

Volund took a moment to decide the Tactical Officer's fate. The Ferret was lucky that the next space dock on HiggramIII was not known for their quality crew replacements. Especially those trained in Gnoll weaponry.

"On screen," Lord Volund snapped through his large feline canines. Gnoll males were powerfully built, like their Earth Lion counterpart. Their shoulders rippled with muscle each time they moved.

The monochrome image of Lord Saga, a fiery female Gnoll, lit up the main comm screen over-looking the bridge. Her golden mane, although not as majestic as her brother's, still had the genetically tinted reflective highlights of the family bloodline that accentuated her jaws.

"Ha, better luck next time, little brother."

"Hrrrumm... You'll get your case of champagne," Volund huffed. Their standing bet was the loser who destroys their prey, bought the other a case of fine Centa champagne.

His sister laughed, her eyes targeting Lord Volund's tactical officer. Grinning she gave him a single clawed paw salute to the air before cutting the connection.

"Comm, contact the convoy to proceed to Antare's Reach. The freighter will need repairs."

Lord Volund sat heavily in his command chair. "Helm, head for Antare's Reach."

"My lord?" they would normally wait for the freighters all to leave first. It was a sign of how angry the Lord felt to break protocol.

Lord Volund waved his paw imperiously.

The Helm turned back to his controls and adjusted the Alcubierre drive (A-Drive). The *Light Bringer's* engines glowed as it twisted away from the freighter and the pirate ship's debris. The bull-nosed frigate sparkled with a green glow that formed from coalescing fireflies of matter that wavered then merged into a protective bubble warping space surrounding the ship. The ship twinkled then disappeared as it dropped into subspace.

◆◆◆

Traynor Lizard Colony

The colony would soon run out of food. Rationing had given them a temporary reprieve. Administrator Shinix stood around the war table, eyeing his advisors. The mysterious disappearance of their food supplies, including the buildings they were housed in, sent chills down the Administrator's spine all the way through his tail.

"Administrator, four ships just entered the system."

"Contact the *Blast'me* to intercept." *Blast'me* was the only Lizard frigate class warship in-system. It was the *only* warship in-system.

Shinix waited impatiently for the intel to come back. "Well?"

"They look to be of Human design. A carrier, a frigate, and two heavily armed freighters."

Shinix sighed.

"Administrator, we have an incoming message. In Lizard! The ships are calling themselves the Terran Navy, a Human military organization. They are offering food and supplies."

"What?!"

"Yes, they are willing to trade food for tech."

Why? They can just take the tech, given the strength of their armaments?

Once again, the Administrator breathed deeply; wondering if this was a reprieve? *If they want to trade, then they're less likely to shoot,* he thought.

Carrier *T.N. Sekhmet*, Traynor System

Admiral Dan Prior sat on the bridge of the carrier *T.N. Sekhmet* and watched the Lizard frigate boost from Traynor III's orbit on an intercept course with his fleet.

Dan looked over to the status board and shook his head. His fleet consisted of four ships, his carrier, a frigate, and two armed freighters. It was all they could spare on this quick mercy dash mission. Yes, they could have transported food directly to the colony, but then the Lizards wouldn't see the strings attached to the aid. Dan was there to show them.

He was surprised that there was only one warship in-system. It had been months since the battle for Earth, he had assumed the Lizards would send for reinforcements.

"Launch both offense and defense fighter squadrons," he ordered. Twelve Astrodevils disengaged from their locking clamps on the outside of the battle carrier and lined up into two formations. Their four ships had now become sixteen.

"Send the prepared message," he ordered. Dan wasn't confident that the trade of food for tech would work. Fiona, the T.N. Interspecies Relations Department Head, had argued that Traynor, as an independent Lizard colony, was far more valuable as a friend under duress than a radioactive hole in the ground. At the very least, Dan mused, they could send Traynor III the Lizard POWs that crowded the camps on Earth.

Chapter 1

Squishy Trade Center, T - 4 hours to Battle for Earth

The door to the conference pool slid open, and three Humans entered.

"Admiral, Commander, Tela is this way," said the soldier as she led John and Jen to seats directly in front of the Squishy alien who soaked in the warm pool.

John could see Tela fidgeted nervously on the stool that rose from the tepid water. His nose tingled as he breathed in the salty, humid air. He had asked to talk to her specifically knowing she was the helmsman of the pirate ship *Kato*. The Squishy Drakmok had let it slip in an interview with an operative from T.N. Intelligence.

"Tela, thank you for seeing us."

Tela's Octopus-like mantel turned a shade of deep green::curiosity::.

Before John could continue, Tela spoke up, her sibilant whisper was translated into a female upper English accent common to BBC presenters. "Are you here to send me back to Cassiopeia."

John looked at Jen before he frowned at Tela. "Should we?"

Silence.

"No, we are not going to send you back. We just seek your advice," Jen said with a smile.

Tela's tentacles relaxed.

The island the Humans allowed them to live on was a paradise compared to the crab infested hideaway that the Pirate Captain Kane used as a base.

Tela had made friends here among the Humans. The females were interesting, practicing many of the things she and other Squishy fems did. Human females had somehow managed to get equal rights to the males, unlike her own culture where they were non-existent.

John cleared his throat and leaned forward. "You've seen many planets in the galaxy. You know what's out there. You also know us, Humans."

Tela nodded at the truth of it.

"We would like your advice on where we should explore, who we should see next?" John asked. The translator on his chest squealed, squeaked and buzzed out his request in the Squishy language. John scrutinized the Squishy but couldn't get any meaningful sense out of reading her body language. He made a note to himself to brush up on his xenobiology. By the look of it, Jen was having the same problem.

"You have a thing that you do here, on Earth, called tourist."

John smiled, knowing that she understood the concept of what he was asking.

"There is no such thing," she said while pointing to the sky with her tentacle, "up there."

"You don't have tourism? But that must be worth trillions or more like quintrillions."

"It is not because they could not, they choose not."

"Are the other species not curious? Surely the benefits of exploring and engaging with other races would be attractive?"

"You misunderstand, they do not because it is too dangerous. It is too easy to be kidnapped, killed or worse enslaved."

John was shocked. Looking to Jen then back to Tela, gauging her belief of its truth. His eyes cast down, his mind circled in thought, wondering if this was why first contact was proving to be so hostile. He was saddened by the news that spacefaring civilizations were, in fact, not very civilized. "Surely there is some sort of peacekeeper up there."

"The main protection a species has is the influence of their Patron."

"I've heard of this term Patron before?" Jen said with her eyebrows raised.

"A Patron is an older, powerful race. Our Patron was the Bear-o'Boar." Tela's mantel changed color so rapidly Jen realized she must have mixed emotions about their protectors.

"The Bear-o'Boar?"

"Yes, a terrible and powerful race. The bears enslaved the Ferrets a century before they found us. We only had Intersolar ships then. Bear-o'Boar claimed us as one of their Servant species. At first, their demands were small, but when they told us to build manufacturing technology to clutter our planet, they demanded more than we could give. They wanted water slaves and mercenaries. They wanted Squishys to kill other soft species from deep oceans."

"What did you do?" John asked, afraid he knew the answer.

"We refused, we fought the Bear-o'Boar." A blue::Sad:: color tinged Tela's mantle. "They destroyed our cities. Many died. Still, we refused, but more Bears came and stole our people to other planets and enslaved all that remained," Tela said as her mantle turned a dark orange::Anger::. Her tentacles twitched. "We are few now."

"Are there other Patrons, better ones?" Jen asked.

"There is the Sil'thik, an insect species or the Choo who are avians. And there's the Ummfact or the Hipp if you like baby minding."

Jen frowned at Tela.

"The Ummfact are small creatures that are good with tools like you Humans. The Hipp are a herd species that have lots of babies. Too many for their worlds."

"So, which are better?" John asked.

"Most of them are not better or worse, but they all have superior technology or thousands of worlds to draw resources from. Some have both," Tela said.

"So none you can recommend," Jen said.

Tela shrugged her fore tentacles. "They are Patrons."

John looked at Jen, her consternation mirrored his at the challenge they had before them.

"Okay, what of those other species you mentioned, the Servant species, the lesser species like the Ferrets?"

Tela shrugged. "There are so many... however, it is complicated. The Servant species have a standing amongst themselves and their Patrons. You are new: you would be put at the bottom of species ranking with the Arboreals. Others Servant species will treat you poorly."

John sat back, his forehead creased. He guessed the Arboreals were some sort of tree life. *So, they would treat us as if we were as smart as some plants? Yay,* John thought. *How insulting.* This was far worse than he had expected. No wonder each species they encountered shot first and talked later. If they survived. John looked at Tela's dark inky eyes, trying to read any deception in them and couldn't. The three talked for the rest of the morning.

"Thank you, Tela, that gives us much to think on."

John and Jen said their goodbyes and headed off. They had what they needed for the UN Security Council briefing. There had been many calls by the public to seek out and partner with other friendly alien species.

John had no such illusions of friendship. Every race they'd come across so far had been aggressive. If Humans could defend themselves, they were better off on their own. What was clear was they needed more intel, which meant going out there. The UN Security Council would not be happy.

The two made their way back to Hope station in orbit. Suddenly sirens blared out a warning. John looked at Jen. They had been expecting the Lizard fleet any day now. Time had run out.

Chapter 2

Rosarito Beach, Baja California, Mexico

The hot, hazy beach was shattered by the roar of four gunboat class spaceships, as they flew overhead along the San Diego coastline. The ships spiraled up and out of the lower atmosphere. That morning's headlines had blazed with another *'Lizard Invasion.'* The ships must have been on their way to fight the aliens. Mags felt guilt slice through her at being on the beach enjoying summer days while the Terran Navy and Earth Forces defended their planet. She could have been doing something, doomsday prepping, stockpiling, anything except sun-baking on the beach with Josh and his best friend, Jake.

Mags stood, shading her eyes to glimpse the vanishing outlines of the ships, the brave souls on their way to war. She gave a silent prayer for the crews to stay safe. On more than one occasion, she had thought about enlisting in the Terran Navy, however finishing her studies would place her in contention for an officer's position. Mags had no doubt that being an enlisted was a waste of her abilities. She had her sights set on something higher.

Mags reverie was broken when Jake tackled Josh heavily to the sand in retribution for some private slight he'd received earlier. Jake was apathetic towards the whole problem of alien contact and the danger that the Earth was in. He seemed to live in a fantasy world without politics, without fear, without thought as far as Mags could detect; which made him boring. At least Josh had an opinion about stuff.

Mags adjusted the pentagram shaped straps of her elegant black swimsuit and sat back down on her towel. The soft crash of the waves drained the stress from her shoulders. The playful grunts made by the two boys down by the water's edge offset the feeling of Zen she usually got from sitting on the beach. Shielding her sunglasses from direct sun, Mags watched the boys wrestle each other on the sand and in the water. Suddenly Josh stopped and looked skyward pointing towards the large explosion that could be seen high above them in the stratosphere. It must've been huge to be visible through the blue hue of Earth's atmosphere. Mags hoped it wasn't the gunships that had previously flown overhead.

♦ ♦ ♦

Near Earth Space – Zero hour, Battle for Earth

Space within near Earth orbit was pierced by lizard nuclear strikes. Squadrons of Human gunboats raced in formation from Earth toward the front lines evading the waves of EM energy pulses. The squat boxlike ships rolled then split off in pursuit of the enormous number of missiles fired from the Lizard war fleet.

The 40 megaton missiles were deadlier than ten Hiroshima bombs. Each was targeted directly at Earth's major cities.

Vice Admiral Jason Dunn had second thoughts about only sending the gunships and any remaining Earth defenses against the myriad of missiles streaking to deliver their deadly payload. The Lizards were decisively winning the battle. Their fleet spearheaded by the battleship marched inevitably toward Earth like a thunderstorm across the bay.

The Human Forces were breaking up against the onslaught of firepower thrust at them by the battleship and its destroyer escort. The sheer firepower thrown by the Lizards was terrifying.

Six small, cargo-container sized weapons platforms held position near the International and Hope space stations. The platforms were set in rapid-fire mode, spewing continuous laser fire at anything that did not broadcast from a friendly transponder.

Admiral Dunn turned to his aide. "Make sure the platforms' computers link to sync with any nearby ships and update their laser targeting."

"Yes, sir." Captain Perry raced off to speak to computer operations.

Jason switched screens to check the status of Hope and the International Space Station's Point Defense (PD); he watched from an onboard vid-cam as the stubby PD missiles launched from their racks targeted the enemy's incoming missile barrage. He could see the reload status slowly change from red to green as another salvo was primed for launch. Jason knew that the ISS and Hope Station were weak points in the defense grid. They were sitting targets. He had tried to have them evacuated but was overruled by their respective governments. Jason gritted his teeth, he had no spaceships left to protect them.

He watched helplessly as the PD missiles destroyed only a handful of the inbound missiles as they passed the stations on their way toward Earth. Several of the Lizard's intelligent missiles veered off to target the weapons platforms, disintegrating them to dust. The remaining eight missiles switched their offensive towards the newly rebuilt ISS. Despite the double layered shields, the 135 crew and scientists aboard the station had no chance. The onboard reactor exploded like a miniature sun killing any chance that there were survivors in escape pods nearby.

Three waves of Lizard missiles flew towards Earth. Land-based plasma cannons fired up at the incoming missiles. The cannons were new technology and were only distributed to the wealthy city-states. Not all the targeted cities on the planet survived the Lizard onslaught.

Rosarito Beach, Baja California, Mexico

Mags picked up her towel and bag, then stuffed all her textbooks and notes inside before she took off towards her car. She had seen enough to change her mind about lazing around on the beach. She had an odd sense of protectiveness towards the Earth that hadn't been there before the first Lizard contact. She now felt an overwhelming need to contribute, to do her part.

Initially, when the alien presence had become public knowledge, she was one of the many students on campus that held a sit-in, holding electric cigarette lighters up demanding peaceful contact by the authorities. How naïve, she thought now. Racing up the beach she dumped her gear on the back seat of her clapped-out second-hand death-trap of a car. In the background, she heard Josh's muffled voice cursing at her. Ignoring him, she jumped in the driver's seat and started the car. The crunch of gears jarred her to release the clutch and force it into gear. Sand sprayed out from the bald tires as the car bolted up the worn track and onto Beach Road heading towards San Diego.

Mags knew that Josh would be able to catch a ride with Jake. She also knew that he would have a few unpleasant words with her because he hated doubling on the back of Jake's trail bike. Especially when he had to grip it with his knees as he held onto two surfboards the whole time. Jake wasn't exactly known for his safe riding skills.

Driving on the side roads, Mags reached the back street entrance of the Rosarito Beach Hotel where they had rented an apartment for the holidays. The rundown two-bedroom unit was in stark contrast to the whitewashed walls of the hotel's facade that dominated the beachfront. Parking her car in the lot Mags walked along the Hotel frontage. She couldn't help but smile at the pseudo-Mexican architectural style of the hotel that to her, came off as tacky. The faded green plastic-coated beach umbrellas with coconut fronds only served to exaggerate the deep red, lobster-colored tourists that littered the beach. She shook her head as she saw hotel guests clinging to the edge of an azure pool, tanning themselves in their pursuit of some imaginary perfection. Wait-staff buzzed around the guests like bees in a meadow of flowers delivering their expensive fruity cocktails.

Once Mags reached their apartment, she gathered her clothes and assorted old fashioned music CDs into her suitcase. Taking a complimentary hotel envelope, she stuffed it with a sheaf of American dollars and wrote Josh's name on the front. She leaned the envelope against a plastic fruit bowl decoration on the table then ran out the door. Back in the car, she made a final mental note to herself to text Josh where she'd left her part of the holiday rental. Unfortunately, she forgot to send the text entirely. That simple act drove an irreconcilable wedge between her and Josh. Their on/off relationship would never fully recover.

Ten minutes later, she was on the highway ticking off items in her mind. The steps of Plan B: finish studies, find a sponsor, get into T.N. Science Division...

♦♦♦

Holiday Accommodation

Jake heard Josh curse at Mags for her total lack of consideration. They both stood frozen as the back of her VW Beetle disappeared up the track trailed by a thin cloud of smoke. Once again, his friend had been left in the lurch. He knew of Josh's fear of riding on the back of his motorbike. His friend hated the idea of passengering; it was a long way to the apartment with a surfboard under each arm. Jake smiled at the possibility of scaring the hell out of him.

Eventually, after several hours in the waves, Josh seemed to dispel all his annoyance with Mags as a smug look danced across his face. Jake had seen that look before when Josh and Mags played practical jokes on each other. Later, in confidence, Josh had told him that the two pranked each other for the sole purpose of make-up sex. It was one of the main reasons Jake was so attracted to Mags; he desperately wanted to experience what Josh had, Mags' soft silky white Goth skin and rich purple lips caressing his.

When the two men reached their rental, Josh got off the bike, his legs almost gave out from holding on tight for so long. Jake claimed the need to pee so strode up the stairs, two at a time and pushed in the door searching for Mags while Josh stayed in the parking lot and cleaned the surfboards. To Jake's dismay, Mags and her gear had vanished. Jake pursed his lips. With Mags gone, there was no chance that he was going to be able to corner her for a drunken anything this holiday like he'd planned.

When Josh finally appeared at the entrance to the rental, Jake had flushed the toilet and was adjusting his shorts. "She's gone, Josh. She's packed her stuff, and high tailed it outa here."

Jake could see Josh's disappointment. "Damn," was all he said.

The two walked around the apartment trying to figure out what to do next. As Josh went to check the bedroom for his girlfriend's things, Jake strode to the kitchen table and picked up the envelope prominently displayed against the fruit bowl. The letter, in Mag's clean rounded script, was clearly marked 'for Josh' on the front cover. Briefly glancing inside, Jake surreptitiously pocketed the envelope.

Jake crossed to the fridge and realized to his delight that Mags had taken off in such a rush that she'd left the best part of a two-day-old pizza still in its battered box. "We got pizza," he said, pulling the box and the last bottle of beer from the fridge, and smiled.

Popping the lid and between gulps, he said matter-of-factly, "Can you buy a case of beer at the store we passed because I got no money on me. I used it all up in gas carrying your sorry ass from the beach."

Josh looked at the empty bottles on the table, and the one in Jake's hand then cursed Mags for not leaving any money.

Mags Apartment, Downtown San Diego

When Mags got home, she slammed the door. She was in a bad mood. Josh had sent her a scathing text for leaving him on the beach in the lurch with Jake to double him back to the holiday accommodations. Then to top it off, leaving him there without the cash to check out.

Mags frowned, confused at his text and sent back she had left money on the table.

Josh texted back, 'don't lie, I hate liars.' He knew Mags must have been short this week because he saw all her newly bought textbooks on the beach. All through the semester, Josh watched Mags constantly skip meals because of her limited funds and the short time available to work. On the summer break, she worked double shifts to make up for it. Josh hadn't seen her around and assumed she was studying because Mags was not a AAA student. It all came down to money. Mags was smart but had to cut classes when she needed money for food or rent. She was currently flush with funds from the extra work during the first half of the Summer break.

Mags saw text after text ping on her phone from Josh. He had just bulled on, accusing her of being a tight-fisted bitch and how he should have listened to Jake when he said she was bad news.

Seething, Mags poured herself a glass of wine then texted him back, *'WTF are you a baby or what?'* She knew exactly what had happened to the envelope of cash she had left on the table. That lying snake, Jake. Mags knew Josh wouldn't believe it of his best friend. He'd been too quick to accuse her; it'd always be a shadow over their relationship. Mags took a gulp of wine and paused, staring at her phone. Then she texted how she couldn't stay because of Jake and what she thought of his friend making sleazy comments on every girl within thirty feet.

It was getting late. So, Mags turned off her phone and logged onto her laptop to flick through her email.

Mag's day tumbled further out of control when an email from her stepmom blinked on the screen. She guessed what it would contain. A not so subtle request for money and a plea for her to deal with her father who had gone out drinking again.

Mag's shook her head. She had had enough. She grabbed the bottle of wine from the fridge and started tapping her response. The words she wrote were brusque, hateful words that admonished her parents for not getting their shit together, and if she'd had the money, she'd have left years ago wiping her hands of the both of them and their dysfunctional relationship. She had disassociated herself from them, from her remaining family. She had written this same email a dozen times, only to let it sit in her draft email folder for weeks until deleting it. However, this time, she took a gulp of wine and pressed send.

Chapter 3

Observation Deck, Max's Station, Titan

John sat at the large viewing window, staring at the swirling methane clouds of Titan below. His stark expression was etched in a grim echo of the fear felt by UN Security Council representatives at their last meeting. The Battle for Earth was over, they had beaten the lizards. Despite all the death and destruction, Earth Forces had rallied behind the UN Consul and nominated John to take them further; to get the intel they needed to settle the question of seeking a Patron or not. John was especially surprised that China had backed the proposal. The death toll in Macau and the surrounding area from the Lizard missile strike ran in the hundreds of thousands.

The decision was, in practical terms, moot since none of the other nations had any interstellar ships. The US had lost their one and only ship in Tau Ceti. Yes, they now had Lizard ships, but nobody knew how to operate them. *Yet.* Many countries had started building ships with what knowhow they had, assuming they would get to add the FTL tech later.

John sat at the window brooding, his mind turning like the chaotic swirl of Titan's atmosphere far below. Under his command, they had won the Battle for Earth, but millions had died. They were still rescuing some unfortunates that were under rubble or caught by tsunamis in the Philippines.

"You know they're right," said a sad but familiar voice behind him.

John looked up to see Jen standing near the glass, her face masked with concern. Her original long hair was cut short, framing her beautiful face, rather than set in a bun; it was a more practical haircut for zero-G.

"Many others could do this..." John started saying.

"No, they can't. You know why. We can't let anybody get their hands on the teleporter technology. If we did, they'd probably kill us all before the end of the day."

John knew she was exaggerating, but the point was valid. In the few T.N. ships that had the teleporter tech, the breakthrough discovery of John's that started it all, a self-destruct was also installed. Except for those few special ships, most jumps or teleports would be made using a centralized jump control center to move new ships or objects. Much like the one destroyed in Tau Ceti.

John and Jen had decided long ago that keeping the use of the transporter capability hidden was an effective way to keep their enemies underestimating T.N.'s capabilities. They would use the slower Alcubierre drive (A-Drive) for FTL travel to hide the fact they also could teleport a ship or object using a J-Drive up to fifty light-years in an instant.

Jen could see John shifting mental gears, his face soured, a frown creasing it in what was becoming a form of habitual self-recrimination.

"What I did to Pete discounts me... I should be locked up for ... crimes against Humanity."

Jen crumpled into the next seat, her eyes blinked red and wet from a flash memory that John's words had evoked. She was still angry at him for giving Pete's brain to Gina so she could experiment with Rezulin.

John's eyes darted to Jen's; he could see the hurt and her angry restraint.

"John, Pete's dead. He would have wanted his body donated to science. It was what he loved," she said with a bite.

"But...," John said.

Jen wrung her hands for the briefest of seconds, then reached forward and held his hand instead. John wasn't surprised their relationship had dulled since the dirty, ghoulish incident had been exposed. He didn't know if it was his guilt or Jen's anger that was rocking their relationship the most.

"Please, John, we need you... *I* need you... to focus on what's before us now and not ruminate on the past. What's done is done."

John looked into Jen's reddened eyes and took a deep breath, closing his own without answering her.

El Paso Research Base, Earth

Jen sat at the large conference table quietly discussing science topics for the upcoming strategy meeting when she spied John enter the room. Capturing his gaze, she saw the doubt in his eyes and gave him an encouraging smile. He looked surprised, but before he could do more than glance at her, he was being hailed by someone further round the table. John was dressed in a smart black uniform with five small silver stars pinned to his collar. He had the striking appearance of a man born to lead.

However, Jen had seen the doubt in his eyes and the tremble in his hands when they were alone.

John chatted with command team members, as he slowly made his way to the head of the table. "Please take your seats. Thank you all for coming. Now that you've had a little time to catch-up, let's get to work. What I'd like to discuss is our strategy going forward from here. Can we first get an update from each of the department heads?"

Admiral Jason Dunn stood facing the extended Command Team. As usual, his uniform was neat and crisp, although he had taken to wearing his hair slightly longer than the regulation length. Acknowledging John, he then said with a clear voice, "As you're aware we've taken a major hit to our personnel and military assets from the last Lizard incursion. We envisage there will be a significant shipbuilding program needed to replace the warships and weapons platforms that were lost. The priority at this stage is one," he counted off on his fingers, "to repair any ships that are easily repaired to battle-worthiness. We were fortunate that none of the shipbuilding yards within the Solar system were attacked directly. Two, I have ordered them to hold new builds until the existing ships are repaired. Half of the UG manufacturing will focus on mines and weapons platforms. There was minor flood damage at the

Indonesian shipyards; however, they should be at full capacity within the week. Three, we will push most of T.N.'s *new* smaller classed vessel shipbuilding efforts out to the colonies. By small, I mean anything less than a cruiser class."

"Do we *have* a cruiser class ship?" someone yelled from the back.

Jason smiled, his hazel eyes brightening. "No, but if we had one, we'd make it here on Earth." A chuckle flittered across the room. "We do have a destroyer and a battleship class." Light murmuring could be heard.

"In your information packs is the Tactics and Strategy group's post-battle analysis with their findings and recommendations; each department's feedback is required ASAP." Jason pointedly gazed at a few Command Team members.

John reiterated, "This is not optional. Get your feedback in quickly." He then waved for Jason to continue.

"We now have five colonies in various stages of deployment. Two are built based on resource collection and processing, two on space tech and ship construction, the last focuses on other world dirtside building construction techniques." He then spoke of the need for a military security review of the colonies.

Jason continued his report as he turned on a holo-presentation listing Lizard warship icons. Each icon was marked with the flag of the nation that claimed them. "Seven, we have a significant number of Lizard prize ships that we'll need to investigate scientifically, then bring them online to battle readiness, and into the T.N. fleet."

Jason spun the holo-presentation above the large table. "In front of you are the classes and numbers of ships, and their approximate times for repair and battle readiness."

John stared at the holograph. "Jason, I see no readiness end date for the Lizard battleship, we need it ready as soon as possible."

"I've had a request by R&D that it should be used for scientific research as opposed to being a war asset to be deployed. In truth, we don't have the staff or expertise to crew all the ships adequately."

John took a deep breath and a moment to think about Jason's reasons. It was true that the ships had priceless scientific value, but they also had a huge military value that could not be overlooked. "I agree that these ships we commandeered from the Lizards have enormous scientific value, and thoroughly exploring and mastering all of the tech they contain would be worth our while," John paused. "However, I still want them battle ready ASAP. We may have won the Battle for Earth, but that was just the start.

I'm afraid of their response to losing a whole fleet. Even a barely operational battleship is a significant deterrent. Jason, we need MIL advisors to help the science teams set the research priority to align with military readiness."

John caught Jason's gaze and held it before finishing.

"This is good work, Jason. You, Thurston and I should have a private conference to determine which ships are to be made available for long-term research."

Both Jason and Thurston nodded.

Jason continued his report. "There has been a scramble for the remaining Lizard warships by Earth Forces. This has caused several incidents involving our claimed ships. Colonel Manders and Director Withers have now assigned extra marines to guard each of our assets."

"Colonel Manders Eric?" John looked around the table trying to spot him. The Colonel stood to take the focus of the meeting.

"In the last battle, we lost a significant number of Marines, approximately thirty-five percent of our total complement. I'm proud to report that their performance in boarding the Lizard warships was outstanding. But there are holes in training we need to fill." The Colonel brought up a holo of a building on an alien world.

"Since the battle for Earth, we've added new ship-to-ship simulations to the Naval Academy's existing planet side training on Titan. I believe by allowing our teams to practice boarding enemy ships and repelling hostile boarders they've been a godsend in the training program. We will be building more of these sims-based enclosures with the different Lizard ship configurations we have access to."

"What were the incidents with Earth Forces on the ships we claimed?" John asked.

"Two scientists, one each from India and Britain who boarded the smaller frigates. One tried for the computers, the other their biomed tech."

John nodded.

"There was also a civilian team from a private corporation."

"Ok...?"

"We sent them home and told them if they were caught again, we would send them home via Alpha Centauri."

Jen stifled a chuckle.

John turned to her sharply and shot her an angry glare, cutting her chuckle short. John suddenly realized his guilt made him abrupt.

Eric continued his report, preferring to ignore the sharp, emotionally charged interplay between his two friends. "Lastly, despite the recent battles, there has been an upsurge in recruitment. We've had to employ quite a few interpreters because the bulk of the new recruits are from non-English-speaking countries. We are looking at ways of implementing the translator's functionality in our suits to augment communication." The Colonel then calmly sat back in his seat.

John turned around the table to the next department head. "Thurston, the state of our corporate and scientific operations?"

The balding and slightly tubby CFO stood and launched into his small presentation.

"Despite all our victories, there has been some media backlash towards T.N. Corporation. Many countries are annoyed that we're keeping the bulk of the Lizard warships and their technology. The battleship Shesha has created the most angst. I've directed the marketing team to coordinate our media blitz, reminding dirt-side that T.N. Corporation *saved their asses* more than once." Someone chuckled in the background at Thurston's uncharacteristic use of the base vernacular.

"We've had to expand our corporate manufacturing structure into areas such as consumables due to the lack of current Human capabilities within that sector."

"Elaborate, please," said John.

"We've started developing space-based manufacturing techniques to assist in making space ready consumables like hairspray. There is a constant shortage of everyday items you would normally find in a grocery store. A lot of these items need to be modified for zero-G; for example, hairspray is now embedded in hairbrushes, so the spray doesn't float forever inside the crew quarters."

"There has been some grumbling in Congress against the size of T.N. Corporation and its growing influence. We are facing anti-trust legislation drafted against us in some countries. For the moment, they are targeting the spacefaring sector and its subsequent subsidiary technologies. This is particularly prevalent in the first world Western markets. Our legal team is taking shape to give them a good fight."

"Monies from the licensing and manufacture of new technologies have continued strongly. Included in your data package is a broad outline of the balance sheet and income statements for the T.N. Corporation. In essence, we are healthily in the black."

Thurston looked over at Jen, who was considered one of their chief scientists. "Science projects in the fields of reverse engineering, civil and military, transport, space-based construction, robotics, and materials have all received extensive budgets. Listed in your packs is the current work in progress. Two new skunkworks are planned: one in El Paso, and the other in Cresseda, on Harmony."

"Lastly, the latest list of gifted technologies to opensource for all are in appendix 4. I need any objections to their release by Friday." An excited hubbub traveled around the room.

John raised his voice to cut through the chatter. "Ambassador Gillard, Interspecies Relations?" John said nodding to her.

"The overall structure of the Department is still fairly dynamic because we are finding out what other species find important. Our interaction with the various new species has fast-tracked our current understanding, which is, unfortunately, still very basic.

"Lizard POW camps now fall under my jurisdiction. The variety of Lizard captives is astounding. Despite their somewhat similar DNA, their bodies and minds are each generally attuned to a specific task." Fiona could see the confusion on their faces. "For example, the fellow S'Sank.

His job was working with the fusion reactors. In his genes, he had greater radiation repair capability built into his cells. It's very helpful if you are working with reactors that leak radioactive substances. Mapping his DNA, we hope, it will lead to interesting possibilities for cell repair in cancer research."

John spoke out. "Lizard brains are wired for the job, so why not their bodies too." Fiona gave John an inquisitive stare. "Gina said as much."

Fiona nodded. "I asked the med team to get sample test DNA for all the Lizards, so we can see what differences there are, and get some insight into what jobs they do. We've had some disturbing results: some of the scans have revealed accelerated organ failure."

John nodded. They had the same results as the *Godzilla* crew when they started to die for no apparent reason. The scientists initially thought it was a virus from the Tau Ceti system, but now John wasn't so sure. "Keep me apprised of their medical condition."

Fiona nodded at his order before continuing. "Many of the Lizard POW camps on Earth are overcrowded. This will need to be addressed soon. Pressure for a quick solution has come not only from the POWs themselves but from governments and popular opinion. There has been an increasing number of media reports of Xenophobia and alien hate versus alien rights groups. So much so, the international court is looking to extend human rights to apply to all sentients." The murmurs from the back of the room highlighted discord within the T.N. ranks. Alien rights was still a hotly debated topic on the talk shows. Some minority groups went as far as to claim that aliens could get more rights than Humans.

"Whatever position the international court decides on alien rights, the hate media against the POWs is becoming all too frequent and influential. We need them removed from Earth for their own protection."

John stared at Fiona, his mind was in turmoil. *He had to become the Lizard protector?* Seriously. He had no love of the scaly cold-bloods, but he didn't want to see any sentient slaughtered out of hand. It would make Humanity just like all the rest of the aliens they'd encountered. Too many humans had died for there to be an easy solution. John sighed, he would have to get them off the planet. The only other solution that crossed his mind was to demystify the infamy surrounding all aliens, especially the Lizards.

Eventually, the meeting wound down, and the Command team headed off to their own departments.

Chapter 4

Adm. Stevenson's office Caladan, Titan

John sat at his desk eyeing the solid man in his early forties. The man's anglo-celtic heritage gave his face a youthful childish appearance around the flushed red cheeks and small clear Harry Potter glasses.

"Who are you, and what are you doing here?" John asked of the man who stood defiantly before him. Off to the side, Bill leaned against some furniture, gauging the rumpled clothes and scarred brown leather carry a satchel. Two armored T.N. marines blocked the door and escape.

Silence.

"He was found sneaking from the AM shuttle airlock near Gate 22 from Hope Station," Bill said.

"Find out who was on duty there and see if we can't patch the hole in security," John said coolly.

Bill nodded.

Turning to the man before him, John looked him up and down. "So, Mr...?"

"You can't unilaterally invade another species' colony. Do you know the consequences of that... it could cause a war that involves the whole of Humanity!" The man jabbered with disgusted outrage, his words coming out in a rush. He blinked rapidly, then straightened his shoulders and his glasses.

John just stared at him, as if he was an interesting type of bug. When he spoke, his voice was coldly impersonal. "Invade a colony, what makes you think we've invaded a colony?"

"I have my sources."

Bill noticed a droplet of sweat slide down the man's temple.

"You're not very smart. Are you," John said caustically. His confidence and calm demeanor seemed to shake the intruder's equilibrium.

"What?" the man said, suddenly unsure of himself. "What do you mean?"

"We don't need to invade a colony to start a war with the Lizards." John moved around in front of his desk until his face was inches away from the intruder. "We're *already* at war with the Lizards!" John said, his voice raised. "I repeat, who are you and what are you doing on my private property."

"The 'Mothers of War' have a right to know..." the man stammered.

"The 'Mothers of War'?"

"The Mothers of soldiers that were MIA, KIA or who actively served."

John stared at the man, trying to decide if he was crazy or for real. He felt for those mothers left behind at home. He also had served in Iraq and seen the changes in his own mother upon his return.

"T.N. can't make decisions for all of mankind... placing their sons and daughters into reckless danger. My article-"

"Oh, I see, you're a reporter."

"The Braidwood Daily News, among other things," the man said with his nose in the air, even as the sweat dripped down his face.

"Bill, take him outside and send him on his way."

As the marines shouldered their weapons, preparing to grab the intruder, the reporter hastily cut in, "I'll get the truth one way or another, the people have a right to know what you lot here in T.N. are doing that impacts us all. You don't have the right to decide for all of us!"

"Airlock 4 or 6?" Bill asked from behind the reporter.

John stared at the man as his face dropped.

"You can't do that!" the intruder cried in disbelief.

"Can't I? Who's to stop me? You're on Titan. Earth laws don't apply here."

"What, no..." the reporter paled.

"Bill, I think, Mr...?" John stepped back as if bringing the interview to an end.

"Lasiter, Gerome Lasiter," the man said crumpling.

"Bill, I think Mr. Lasiter will be co-operative?"

"Yes, I will."

"Mr. Lasiter wants to see Traynor... we should show him," John said.

"Has the food skirmish slowed?" There had been reports of infighting and hoarding by lizards on Traynor III when it became apparent that not all would survive till supplies arrived from the Empire.

"What skirmish? Is there one at Traynor? Where on Earth is Traynor?" Lasiter butted in.

Bill glanced at the reporter. "Mostly. We can't guarantee his safety, it's too dangerous."

"And the food transports? We have the second delivery on the fifth of March."

"Food?" the reporter echoed.

"Humanitarian aide of Lizard food sent to Traynor Colony. It seems you have a lot to learn Mr. Lasiter," John said. "Bill, will you see to it that he's delivered to dock 3?"

Bill looked at John with a raised eyebrow, then after a moment nodded.

Mr. Lasiter's face paled further.

Bill sidled forward grabbing Lasiter's shirt collar in one quick motion. "C'mon, time for you to go on a little trip."

"If he doesn't change his mind, you know what to do."

Lasiter gave John a baleful look.

Five days later, the reporter walked sullenly down the corridor. His face pale and drawn from the experiences he'd seen on his trip to Traynor colony. Even with his marine escort, the reporter had a newfound respect for the T.N. and the man that led them. Just as he thought his adventure was over, and that he would be sent back to Earth, he was summoned to report to dock 7. The *T.N. Grace* was being resupplied in preparation to disembark.

♦♦♦

Dock 7

Jen and John strolled down the corridor towards *Grace's* hatch. Waiting there were two armed marines and a scruffy looking man standing meekly between them. John looked over at Jen when they arrived.

"Jen, this is Mr. Lasiter. He's concerned about the Human invasion of alien colonies. He'll be coming with us on a quick trip to Cresseda to gain more insight as to what T.N. is on about; protecting Earth and protecting Humanity," John said deliberately as he stared at the reporter. He could see Lasiter's jaw clenched, ashamed at his behavior in their earlier meeting five days before. After the tour, Bill had reported his positive reaction to the mounds of food delivered to Traynor. And that he was just as mystified as the lizards as to where their original food stocks disappeared to.

Jen frowned at the untidy rumpled looking man, but before she could ask a question, Mr. Lasiter squirmed away from his marine guard and held out his hand.

"It's an honor to meet you, Ms. Gale; I've heard so much about the Guardian Angels. My daughter would be chuffed if you could sign this book for her." Somehow the man had extracted a book from his bag with the title *'Guardians or Greedy Pariahs.'*

"I don't think so, Mr. Lasiter," Jen said, eyeing his hand as if it were a poisonous snake. "We've been given enough grief by the press for saving the world. If you don't like our methods, *write a book.*"

John was surprised at Jen's sarcastic tone. His eyes shifted to the spine of the book Lasiter was holding, 'International best-selling author, G. Lasiter.'

Mr. Lasiter seemed chastened by Jen's quick pick up.

John turned to his ever-present escort and asked them to escort Mr. Lasiter to the passenger compartment in the rear of the vessel. "We will be launching in ten minutes," he said as they departed the main lock.

"This way, Mr. Lasiter, we'll get you bedded down," said Sgt. Bull.

The reporter watched over his shoulder as the two Guardian Angels turned and headed for the bridge.

"John!" Jen shook her head in dismay. "Why would you sanction a visit by such a jerk? What is going on?"

John's neck flushed red. "I didn't know he was a bestselling author, I thought he was just a small-town reporter."

Jen bit her bottom lip. She hated the papers because they printed such spurious and cruel things about T.N. and worse about the daughters of the Taken. There was no doubt in her mind the media had their share of ignorant, self-serving reporters, journalists, and so-called experts, all trying to make their own reputations and cash out of the situation.

It didn't help that Evie was still in court over royalties for her new Liz and Puff dolls. Owners of the dolls could dress them in changeable skins. Some skins were human-like, whereas others were discolored lizard scales. There was even a pullout hook on the bottom to attach a spiked tail.

Civil libertarians and alien rights activists were in an uproar with calls for an entity rights act that included human-lizard half-breeds. The call fell on deaf ears. For now, a fascinated public watched the reality court show like a ticking time bomb, as if nothing else mattered.

Jen sat at her console, waiting for him to continue.

"I thought that if he saw the truth, and reported on some good things we're doing, it would ease the hate mail."

"John, nothing can erase what you did to Pete. No newspaper article, no confession, nothing will erase that blight."

Jen was mildly surprised to see John's eyes widened as he heard the bitterness in her voice. She realized that he mustn't have noticed it before.

Jen turned away and started her preflight check. "Lasiter's *your* responsibility, I want nothing to do with him."

In the corner of Jen's vision, she saw a sad look on John's face as if he had been punched in the gut. When she turned to face him properly, he had turned away and was making his own checks. She noticed his neck was flushed red with emotion.

Chapter 5

Coronado Beach, San Diego

Mags parked the car just off route 75, a short walk for her and the boys across the road to the white sandy beach. Autumn breezes billowed from the Pacific Ocean up and over the peninsula that formed San Diego Bay. Down off the main road, US navy flyers from the Naval Air Station ran training drills over the dunes and beach. The sailors in their black T-shirts and coverall matching camouflage blues were a stark contrast to the day-tourists with their gaudy fluoro-colored swimwear.

Mags wrinkled her nose as she jerked her head back from the rancid smell of old coconut suntan lotion she had inadvertently used to lather her arms. The thick gooey cream was all that was available in the dilapidated grocer near her apartment. As she stood on the beach staring out to sea, the smell triggered old memories of her childhood where her birth mother covered Mags and her sister in the same coconut suntan cream. The three of them had played in the fine white sands of Sydney's northern beaches. Small pockets of spinifex grass grew through the reclaimed sandy dune peaks. Down by the water's edge, Mag's elder sister, Jen, built magical worlds where Princess' lived as prisoners within turrets of elaborate seaweed encrusted sandcastles. Mags scowled, then shook her head destroying the hot sun-induced memory. Those days were long gone, she fretted.

Thoughts of her older sister, the sister that had abandoned her, shattered her happy mood. Inevitably her mind drifted again to ponder on her birth mother. She had very little recollection of her, except a warmth that coalesced around her like a winter blanket. She had been five when one day her mother just disappeared in the surf. Then, as if in a trance like the wispy dance of a whirlwind, Mags' life tumbled in freefall towards a father she'd only heard about in ugly late-night whispers. She had barely gotten used to her mom's absence and father figure when she tumbled again. She had turned to her stalwart sister who, not long after disappeared as well. She had been the only other real thing in her life. Jen had bailed on her, leaving her to a scary father and hairy stepmom she didn't know.

Her father met Jazmine before he'd separated from Mag's birth mom when she was a baby. Her new stepmother refused to talk about her birth mom and sister; the devil sister who had run away and the mother, who'd deserted her. Often her father would cite their crimes, and with repetition, any mention of her birth mom and sister became poisonous. Inside, the loneliness clawed at Mags throughout her childhood.

Her new stepmother, treated her like the daughter she could never have, spoiling her just as she pleased. Mags, at an early age, suffered indignities brought on by her new mom's pandering. She would dress Mags in pink princess' outfits. At first, walking the catwalk in barbie outfits was a novelty. But by the age of eight, the shocking pink and mock pastel clothing made the catwalk parade a carnival attraction. Eventually, with dreary repetition, her world became a wearisome insufferable reality. Each new glossy outfit bore a satanic religious resemblance to the venerable Barbie and Ken dolls. Jazmine dressed Mags in the gaudiest mismatched outfits worn by the dolls, and all too often the buff Ken. By the age of ten, Mags hated the plastic dolls and their outfits with a passion. One day in an act of gleeful frenzied revenge, she gathered all the dolls in the house and savagely hacked off their heads with a rusty garden machete. Jazmine grounded her for a month, which suited Mags just fine. She had school assignments to do.

Her new mum had a terrible and vindictive temper which was marginally better than her overprotective generosity. She could still hear Jazmine's drawl, "...but honey, I'm only doing it for your own good. Sweetie Pie." Mags knew now that Jazmine had been afflicted with a terrible bi-polar disorder that sent her on roller coaster mood swings. She would bounce from up on high to the depths of depression.

By her mid-teens, her usually apathetic father was an intermittent disciplinarian. His strong arm always seemed to manifest itself after a dozen cold beers. Initially, he had found Jazmine's mood swings quaint until they interfered with his pub nights. Then all hell broke loose, and Mags made herself scarce.

By the age of sixteen, she realized that she had grown up alone. Living in fear and battling Jazmine's mood swings that were counterbalanced by more and more regular unsolicited disciplinary beatings from her father. The daily challenge began in the morning with the dread of trying to negotiate with her family dynamic. Moving out of home at the earliest possible moment, away from all the drama, she knew was the only way to stabilize her life.

Once away, Mags consciously built a new persona to seek out something better, something that was not so painful. She was intelligent like her sister, so her grades at graduation saw her offered scholarships to more than one college. She gratefully accepted a biochemistry scholarship from the University of San Diego several states away from her parent's influence.

At college, Mags kept much of her tragic home life private. She gravitated towards darker things, exploring gothic life and fashion styles to hide her inner scars. Her face bore the traditional white mask hardened by tragic circumstance. The dark eyeliner and purple accented black hair helped disguise the real Mags. She could expose as much or as little as she pleased, which typically meant only a special few saw through to her real character. College rumor branded her a gothic witch. Unexpectedly, it meant her choice of friends was focused around the ostracized, weird or dangerous. Mags slowly healed with time and trips to the beach.

Mags stared at the horizon, her left hand shading her eyes from the glare of the sun. Her strapless black swimsuit emphasized her lily-white skin despite her recent trips to the beach.

The two boys surfed like maniacs, chasing elusive waves with their tri-fin boards. She closed her chemistry textbook with a sigh; she was not going to get any more study done today. She had set off in the break with her friends intending to mix study with a little sun and surf. A simple, relaxed lifestyle surrounded by a few friends and perfect weather tipped the scales towards lazing about versus judiciously preparing for the next term's harder units on campus. It was Autumn now, and her thoughts revolved around moving to the Uni campus for the remaining semester.

After that first summer break, her relationship with Josh was damaged. Jake had seen to that. So now, she only let him into her world at arms-length despite their relationship do-overs. The on-off fling she was having with him made studying that much harder. He would irritate her with the ease that he passed exams and sailed through his own study units. She knew that he would someday become a brilliant mathematician, which bothered her more than she would like to admit. Just yesterday he'd caught her reviewing her notes while at the beach.

"What's with the books Mags? Studying again?"

"Just want to get a little ahead."

Josh pulled a fifty dollar note from his wallet and held it out to her. "Get us some crisps, will you?"

Mags stared at the note. Ever since the disaster holiday, Josh had gone out of his way to pay for everything with large notes just to annoy her.

Just as he couldn't get past the stealing, she couldn't get past him accusing her of freeloading.

How dare he! She'd always paid her dues, ever since she was a child. By the age of ten, she had gone to work in the local supermarket stacking shelves just so that she could pay for a decent meal every so often for her family. Her father, when he did work, was very well-paid; so money really wasn't an issue. Until her new stepmother started on a downward spiral of collecting credit cards. The accumulated debt eventually fractured their family. Bitter fights broke out between her father and stepmom. So, Mags paid her dues.

Josh had black, shoulder length hair that highlighted his lanky build and whiter than white skin. He always seemed to get sunburnt despite heavy sunblock. His lack of tan made him an ideal match for Mags' goth image, except when he turned lobster red.

So today Mags watched Josh and Jake dance between their beach towels and the surf as the scorching sand scalded their feet. The two raced out of the water and up the beach where Mags tried to sunbathe surrounded by her scattered textbooks.

"Josh," Mags complained as salty wet sand dripped off his surfboard to land squarely onto her books and copious freehand notes. Josh was taken by surprise when Mags grabbed a fistful of sand, balling it, and threw it aiming for his head. Ducking while holding his board, Josh slammed his surfboard into Jake's crown jewels; much to Mag's delight. She never liked Jake; she suspected he stole her rent contribution from the last holidays. It just couldn't be proven. Jake argued that Mags hadn't left any money or if she had, he suggested the maid had stolen it. Even now, it was a sore point between her and Josh because he paid for it all. Besides that, Jake was always trying to hit on her despite Josh being his best friend and her warnings of grievous bodily harm.

Giggling, she took off to avoid Josh's sandy retaliation. Mags eventually returned to her towel after been chased to the water's edge with Josh's own wet sand ball.

◆◆◆

University of San Diego

When word of *first contact* leaked out and that the American government had fired upon the first demonstrable contact with a UFO, there was a massive outcry. Mags was among them. She demonstrated against the authorities for taking such an aggressive stance. Unknown to the world, the 'UFO' was John, Jen, Max, and Elvis, flying in the first jump ship the *Scotty*.

Then came the first Lizard incursion with devastating results. Mags had just finished her undergrad degree in biochemistry to start her masters when the 'Guardian Angels' started to appear in space near Earth regularly.

Two tiny alien ships that were acting as protectors were all that stood between Earth and the big bad galaxy. The alien mass abduction at El Paso had first been shrouded in mystery; however, on its exposure human angst towards aliens had crystallized.

Demonstrations of Xenophobia against all Aliens became ugly and violent. Even the Guardian Angels had an infamous reputation. When the Angels finally revealed themselves as Humans from the T.N. Corporation Mags, like the rest of the world, was stunned but relieved. The video produced by the Corporation left no doubt that they were protecting the Earth. It raised serious questions within Mags's mind as to the relationship between the US government and the T.N. Corporation. She was not the only one. She spent the time to find out more about the now famous Corporation. How had they built two spaceships without the rest of the world having the smallest inkling?

The damning accusations by the T.N. Corporation that the US and Chinese governments had attempted to hijack the Guardian Angel spacecraft awoke feelings of shame and utter disbelief at how amoral her own government had acted.

What chilled her to the core was the revelation of the mass abduction by the Lizards, not for their technical expertise or even their ability to create art. It was much baser than that, the simple requirement to eat. People were Human cattle to the Lizards. This made her angrier than she had ever been. Not only did she want to join T.N., but she became a vegan.

Mags' last year of her masters was a very busy year. In the end, she had to break off her relationship with Josh and burn it down. If he couldn't get past the holiday trip outside of San Diego, then Mags would be standoffish to protect herself. The feeling of liberation made it that much easier to disparage Jake and stave off the slug's not so subtle attention. It seemed to her, they were becoming monotonous in their regularity; every time Josh wasn't around. When she approached Josh and suggested his best friend wasn't a friend at all because he was thwarting their relationship, Josh accused her lab partner of the selfsame thing. Mags was taken by surprise at Josh's jealous streak. Then she noticed the whispered words and the secretive childish laughs between Josh and Jake. Why Josh couldn't see his friend's duplicity was a mystery to her. By the end of the term, it didn't matter because she broke it off.

Mags devised her exit plan. Subtle changes in her tweaked an uncharacteristic social conscience with a need to protect Earth against alien invaders. She would, in a few more months, finish her studies, and then apply to the Terran Navy for a science position within the officer traineeship scheme. She knew that any posting would probably send her further afield than downtown San Diego. They had a base in Australia, which suited her; it was far enough from Josh and his toxic friend, Jake.

Chapter 6

City Heights Apartments, San Diego

Mags dumped her books and datapad on the bed. She had been to SDSU to drop off her final paper for her bioscience masters. The last units had been grueling since she packed in her restaurant job and gym workouts around her study timetable. Back in her first year, bullying from louts near where she lived forced her to take up self-defense for her own security. She couldn't afford to live on campus, so making the trek to the university had its challenges. She kept to herself, avoiding the obvious gang influences. Her Goth persona didn't help against street thugs.

Mags pulled out her laptop and opened her mail.

She smiled at the message that appeared in front of her. She received confirmation of employment from the Terran Navy. The email specified packing for a ten-day trip. Recruitment agencies had been canvassing the universities, including SDSU, for innovative academics that sought adventure to see the galaxy. Well, that's what the marketing hype said. At least she'd be able to get out of her slumlord property.

There it was in black and white pixels. There was her escape plan and her future at T.N. It had been an arduous last few years, but Mags was thrilled that she had reached this far without any help from her parents. Not that she would've accepted it. She sent a very succinct email to her stepmother and wondered if it would end up in Jazmine's spam folder. Ever since her drunken facts of life email to her parents, their relationship had been more strained, if that was possible. Mags did feel some guilt, especially for those earlier years after her sister had run away, leaving Mags to fend for herself against a family of dire wolves. The love-hate relationship she'd had with Jazmine was tumultuous, but she'd been there, unlike her sister or birth mother.

Mags showered and put on her one and only two-piece suit she used for special occasions. Black with purple highlights matching her hair stripe. Stifling a smile, she grabbed her heavy duffel bag, pentagram necklace with amethyst crystal insets and headed out to T.N.'s offices on 6th Ave in downtown San Diego.

♦ ♦ ♦

"Margaret Hanks," a tall, lanky fellow said as he directed her and several other specialists from the main foyer. Mags nodded in his direction gaining his attention.

The man counted the heads before him then took off towards the staff entrance at the back of the room, "Follow me," he said over his shoulder.

Quickly the six picked up their bags and chased after the rapidly disappearing figure.

Once through the double doors, the man continued at a breakneck pace. Mags was glad she wore her Doc Martin's, they were better than the black spidery stilettoes she had planned to wear.

"You are being assigned to the research arm of T.N. Corporation. However, you will all need to complete the physicals to determine where the bosses think you will be useful. Here are your certification LCDs, where you will record your qualifications, including your physical. Here is a list of your first certificates you will need to pass *before* you can move up in the company." The LCD screen card had a clip to attach it to clothing. On the left side was her head as a holograph ident. Mags glanced at their guide's chest where she saw his certificates, a myriad of colored lights showed on its surface.

Mags's eyes widened as she scanned the list of required basic certifications that went on for two pages.

"Wait a minute," the solid, balding man of the group said. "I'm here for the intraspecies immunology, not some physical or this thing called Basic."

Mags scanned down to Basic, it was broken down into Mil, Space, Dirt, and EVA. They were all required courses and, 'OMG' she thought, awed, some of them were located on *Titan*.

"Everyone does the physical and basic, no exceptions. That was explained in your interview."

"Well, yes. I thought that was on Earth, not Titan." the man spluttered, "I can't go into space. So, I don't need to take the physical."

"Dr. Reynolds, there is a war on. Either do as I say or there's the door. Maybe one of the other Navies will take you."

"But I thought ... I didn't join the Navy. I joined T.N. Corporation."

The lanky man stood fast, then sighed, "What do you think T.N. stands for?"

Dr. Reynolds stared blankly for a moment then slowly picked up his bag and headed for the door.

"Does anybody else have second thoughts?"

Mags looked at each of the others in her group. Scanning the skills covered in Basic, it looked like army boot camp. She had seen old movies on it where the characters all needed to work together and to trust each other in the end. Could she trust the faces that surrounded her? No doubt she will need to rely on them when she goes through this thing called Basic: Dirt, on Titan.

The lanky man pointed to a door at the end of the corridor, "OK. In through there, you'll find lockers for your things, overalls and specimen jars. The doctor and nurse there will direct you." The man turned and headed off through another door and was gone.

"I guess this is it," Mags said as she held her hand out. "My name's Margaret, but everybody calls me Mags."

◆◆◆

It had been ten weeks of physical and mental testing; Mags was exhausted. The group lost two and gained another four from a separate induction. Mags did well on the physical tests from all the time she had put into self-defense. The instructors gave her increasingly more difficult challenges, often separating her from the rest of the team, only to wind back with them in the evening.

"Hanks, Saunders, Hoff, and Bauman. Grab your gear and git to the next shuttle on platform seven, you're going to Titan for the start of your Basic."

Mags looked at the others with trepidation. They had all heard the stories of Basic – Dirt around the mess hall. Unlike militaries on Earth, T.N. trained their crew in all manner of conditions on different planets, in space and on moons. The Titan surface was a notorious hellhole of frozen methane storms that rained rocks as big as your fist, and volcanic flows of cyanide lava.

Mags entered the shuttle with her three colleagues. Each took a seat, waiting to be briefed on safety in a space shuttle. The check-in and terminal staff made the whole experience surreal, like taking an international flight, as if going to space was no big deal. Mags sighed, pinching herself, this was her new reality.

Mags was interrupted by an elderly man taking the seat next to her. "Miss Hanks?"

"Yes?"

"I'm Dr. Basheer. I'm heading up a new project in the Bio-Science division of T.N. I have requested you join my staff once you complete your basic training."

"Doctor, it's nice to meet you. I studied your work on proto-plankton, it was brilliant. You asked for me?"

"Thank you, yes. I've been watching your career for a few years now."

Mags got a distinctly uncomfortable feeling, like being stalked. "Oh..." Suddenly it dawned on Mags, "You sponsored me for the job." Somebody had, and she was sure as hell it couldn't be her family. She had suspected her tutor at university, but the lecturer denied it. Mags shook her head, no, not her alcoholic father nor her Bimbo Barbie mother or her missing in action sister.

A smile skimmed across the Doctor's face. "Yes."

"I don't know what to say," Mags was flustered for the first time in a long time. "Why?"

"Your mother asked me to keep an eye out for you," he said quietly.

"Jazmine... but?"

"She did something for me a long time ago, that I'll never forget."

Mag's eyes narrowed. "What does she want?"

"Nothing. Jazmine asked me not to tell you of the sponsorship, but I couldn't hold that back in all conscience." Mags knew how big a deal it was for the doctor to stick his neck out for her sponsorship. Jazmine must have done something *really* special for him.

Suddenly the seatbelt sign flashed on as the engines roared to life drowning out any other sound, which suited Mags. Her mind reeled in turmoil, her body suddenly stiffened as she was pressed into her seat. The deck gravity fell away as the shuttle angled skyward pulling two G's and climbing. Turbulence buffered the small shuttle in Earth's atmosphere until it suddenly ended and the shuttle passed into space leaving some passengers shell-shocked. Mag's hair stood on end as zero G took hold. They were truly bound for Hope Space Station. Her stomach did a somersault as her body tried unsuccessfully to establish the real up and down. Mags turned green.

"First time in space?" Dr. Bashir asked with a smile on his face.

Mags nodded. She didn't want to talk to him now. Despite nausea from the flight, he'd set a bomb off amid her emotions. *And he's talking like it's a change in the weather.*

♦ ♦ ♦

Hope Space Station

Mags heard a clunk as the ship docked and the grav plating started to draw power from the station. The plates were high tech but power hogs. Her body eased into her seat, settling her stomach and inner ear.

"New T.N. employees, follow the green line to baggage control," the flight attendant said as she assisted people off the shuttle and onto Hope Station.

People bustled excitedly through the airlock of the transport and into the softly lit corridor leading to the terminal area. Mags couldn't help but notice the non-tourists moved with an urgency borne from expedience. Many wore T.N. navy uniforms with military insignia and military ratings.

"Sir, Ma'am, please move on, you're blocking the bot."

Mags was caught by surprise when a Marine in space armor stepped out from near the shuttle entrance ring. The black and grey breast plating had some deep parallel scratches that looked like claw marks.

"Sorry," Mags said as she stepped aside to let a wheeled bot with supplies move through. She could hear Hoff next to her complain under his breath at the need to move for a robot, it should wait for Humans, not the other way around.

Mags could see the Marine grimace but held his tongue. Turning toward the quickly disappearing bot, she saw it had a red cross on its side; it must be carrying med supplies. Yet another raw reminder of the recent battle with the Lizards.

Mags followed a multitude of stripes that were painted on the floor. Colored arrows in the lines gave directions to the main facilities. The newbies walked down the docking corridor to the main colonnade where there stood tall reinforced curved bulkheads that framed the full length of the outer walkway like roman columned archways. The group passed colored hatchways that let to other docking bays named after companies such as Galactic Spaceline or Westons Express Freight. LCD screens adorned the apex of each arch displaying the name of the docked ship and its destination.

Several bays along, Mags watched as a detail of Marines escorted three officers out of a private T.N. bay. Their smart black dress uniforms made them stand out against the black matte plated armor worn by the Marine guard. Onlookers respectfully made way for the group as they swaggered on towards a blocked off Military zone.

Four more marines guarded the checkpoint allowing a young officer to check their identities as they waited patiently.

"Admiral, the U.N. Consul is in the Capetown meeting room."

"Thank you, Lieutenant. Please tell him I'll be there shortly. Have the chef prepare something for all of us, I'm sure the consul will be hungry."

"Yes Sir," the Lieutenant said then threw a sharp salute and rushed off down the corridor.

Then without formality, the female officer hugged the Admiral and kissed him goodbye to rush off down the corridor in the opposite direction trailed by two marines.

"Did you see who that was?" Hoff whispered in Mags ear. "That's the big boss. They say he's got balls of steel cause he gave his friend's brain to the Lizards. Personally, I don't believe it... it's so much marketing hype to counter the goody two shoes 'Guardian Angel' reputation, it's gotta be ..."

Mags couldn't help but watch the female officer race off into the distance.

♦♦♦

Training Ground, Titan Surface

"Oh, crap." Mags strained within the confines of her spacesuit. Bending at 45 degrees and pumping her legs to spring, she jumped high in the low gravity to avoid the large fissure that had suddenly opened before the group. Mags grunted as she landed on all fours, winding herself. Breathing heavily, she slowly stood, straightening the kinks in her tired muscles. The durable space suit had a remarkable range of movement, allowing some jumps to be robotically assisted. The extra power only worked if you took the training. An annoying flashing icon warned her that the exoskeleton assist was still engaged. Mags stood bent gasping, the assist helped, but it was still damn hard work trying to control and coordinate it. Too much push could send her tumbling off course and out of control or worst, crash landing inside a fissure.

Abruptly her helmet comm crackled with the sharp, rough gravel of their instructor "Cadet Leader Hanks, what the hell are you doing?! Get your group over to Monkey Head on the double!"

Mags had been given temporary command of the six-person group. Apparently, there was no such thing as a democracy when frozen methane hailstones the size of a man's fist fall from the sky. They can kill in an instant. Sergeant Kahn had taken a shine to Mags and her superior physical ability, so promptly gave her twice as much work. It was one-time Mags just wanted to be one of the crowd.

Breathing hard, Mags pulled herself atop the small rocky outcrop. Adjusting her satellite topographic map with physical terrain visual so she could see the ground ahead. It had changed since the morning exercises. The Titan surface was like that, an ever-shifting continental Pangaea, like the staircases in Hogwarts but deadly.

Mags tapped her squad-only channel selector. "Hoff, you need to head south two clicks then follow the ridge."

"Oh, man, do we have to go that far?"

"Hoff, we don't have time for your crap, you need to get moving pronto." Mags couldn't keep the frustration out of her voice. The man was a consummate lazy sac. Leave him for five minutes, and he'd be snoring in the corner.

Mags looked out over the icy frozen wasteland of Titan's surface. Clouds were forming in the distance. The Sarge was right; they needed to get moving before the weather front moved in. They couldn't afford to get caught out in the hailstorm.

◆◆◆

Back in her apartment at the base, Mags held her cert badge up to the light. It was a multicolored LED that displayed her completed certifications or ratings as some like to call them. Smiling, she saw the tri-colored patch for Basic Mil, Space, Dirt and EVA ratings. Titan offered so much more than she could get back on Earth. The Navy was a training powerhouse. Her last certifications were in hand-to-hand combat. Sgt. Kahn had pushed her to try for them just to keep her fit.

Now, she needed to concentrate back on her studies, back on biology. She leaned over and dialed Dr. Basheer's comm to set up a meeting.

"Miss Hanks. I was getting worried you had changed your mind," Basheer said. "I was apprehensive that my mentioning your mother had ..." The doctor seemed genuinely contrite at mentioning her mother's involvement in Mag's career.

"No, it took me by surprise, that's all."

"Good. I guess you have called to join our team?"

"Yes, sir."

"My shuttle is due in on Friday 0600TST, so how about we meet at noon in Cafe Lyon on deck oh-seven where we can discuss it over lunch."

"Ok, I'll be there."

"Excellent," the Doctor said, then cut the connection.

Mags sat back in her chair and took a deep breath. The training over the last four months had been rigorous and exhaustive. A small completion ceremony was scheduled for the afternoon shift.

When Mags arrived at the Cafe, she met up with the other team members of the E Project Biology group. Dr. Basheer explained that the team was tasked with research on the biodiversity of other planets or lack thereof. It seemed the majority of the planets visited by the interstellar probes had found limited sustainable life. Earth's diversity was the exception rather than the rule.

The group was charged with visiting new worlds to formulate theories on biodiversity. Everyone knew of the incredible benefits that a biosystem made to new discoveries, especially to medicine. There was an expectation that there would be a similar benefit from the alien worlds visited.

The second priority was to make sure that Earth was protected from contamination from other worlds. They didn't want to inadvertently bring back nasty pests or micro-organisms to Earth who would have no natural defense against them.

Chapter 7

Australian Outback, Lizard POW Camp

John and Rezulin followed the armed soldiers into the main yard of the Lizard POW camp. A group of a dozen Lizards mingled near the double gated entrance of concentric triple electrified fencing that surrounded the camp. John stared at the Lizards that looked sickly; they were drawn and listless, aimlessly mingling along the fence boundary.

He could tell they were suffering withdrawal symptoms, probably from their jobs. Shaking his head, John wondered again at the horrendous practice of genetic imprinting of a person's job on their DNA. Not doing their job was killing them. What could be worse? John thought they seemed lost without their ships and their jobs onboard. Slavery came to mind but was dismissed just as quickly; they were a different species.

A path opened up when smaller lizards respectfully moved aside for the large lizard with a purple flaming tattoo that walked towards the two visitors.

"War Leader... Rezulin?" Darvus queried, confused. He had sent Rezulin back to Traynor Colony to repair the *Godzilla*, and now he was here, in the POW camp with the Human jailers.

"Lord Darvus," Rezulin said before dipping his head in respect. "This is Fleet Admiral Stevenson."

Darvus focused an appraising eye over John.

"Few species fight as well as the Humans, fewer are as stupid."

John looked to Rezulin with a raised right eyebrow.

"He means many species fear the Lizard Empire and would not fight, they would run."

"Humans are not like other species," John said, although it seemed a hollow statement. Maybe they should have run. "Your crews grow weak in the camp?" John said as he pointed at two Lizards that sat in the open staring into space.

"There is not enough stimulation here," Rezulin said.

Darvus cocked his head like a bird assessing its prey.

"Why do you not kill us now and end our suffering!"

Surprised, John said, "Is that what you expect?" Waiting for a response, he looked between the two Lizards. Darvus was serious; Rezulin, he wasn't so certain of because of his inscrutable facial expression.

"Most species expect death or slavery after being beaten," Rezulin said without feeling; his eyes focused on the Fleet War Leader.

John stood there, contemplating Rezulin's words. Earth had had its share of dark history, including genocide and slavery. It was sad to see Tela's words were the galactic norm. John turned to Darvus. "Humans have a tradition not to kill prisoners."

Darvus sighed. "Slavery then."

"There is another matter," John said as he scrutinized the two lizards near the wire staring into the distance. His mind twisted at an extraneous thought, *The under stimulation of the cold-bloods. They need to do something.*

John shook his head to focus before he pressed on with his proposal. "Teach us Lizard tech, then we will give you political asylum, universal entity rights and settle you on a new world." John waited for what he thought was an obvious choice.

Earlier John had spoken to Rezulin about the concept of political asylum and universal entity rights. He explained that *'In essence, Humanity, through the international criminal court, accorded the same Human rights to all intelligent species, making the Lizards in captivity prisoners of war rather than animals to be slaughtered.'* He wasn't sure if Rezulin believed him that Humans practiced such a thing or that Humans could protect Darvus from their brethren. Normal Lizard protocol expected the loser to gracefully die or be enslaved. Neither choice seemed very palatable to John.

After a very one-sided conversation, John left Rezulin in the POW compound to convince the old Fleet War Leader of the sincerity of John's offer.

When the two War Leaders were alone, Darvus turned on Rezulin. "Traynor Colony, was it attacked?"

Snorting, Rezulin blinked and looked at Darvus sideways. "Yes. These Humans get around."

"Traynor has fallen...?"

"I don't know. We were taken out of the fight at the beginning."

Darvus nodded.

"Why did you come?" Rezulin asked.

Darvus cocked his head to the side as his eyes narrowed at Rezulin, "To Earth... That's an obvious question..."

"No, why did *you* come, and not another Fleet Leader? Your clan has no businesses with ours."

Darvus stood still. "The Heretics. The non-believers have infiltrated the Empire everywhere."

Lizards acquire the DNA of the food they consume, including all its junk genes. Heretics believe in retaining old DNA and not cleansing it after eating a foreign sentient species. What DNA was cleansed was decided by the Inquisitors. In practical terms, inquisitors regularly killed Heretics when they found them rather than exorcise unwanted gene fragments. The inquisitors cemented their power by ritualizing the cleansing process making their selections divine providence and the will of the creator.

Rezulin nodded his understanding, then thought a moment. "You believe there are Heretics in the Unak Clan, in Traynor Colony." Rezulin paused. "How many did you arrest and kill?" Rezulin recalled the Governor speak of Darvus ordering the killing of a few lizards.

Darvus started, surprised that Rezulin deduced as much.

"Twenty-two in Traynor, plus their base in Graylon 3." (Tau Ceti was the Human name for the system).

Rezulin flinched. That was his crew that he watched getting slaughtered in Tau Ceti from a Lizard orbital bombardment.

Darvus' tongue flickered as he tasted the air, then he smiled with an eerie blank stare at Rezulin. "You're going through *pildak*?" he stated.

Rezulin nodded, it was the process of Lizard brain DNA transition from eating another species brain.

"What species did you eat?"

"Human."

Darvus' grin broadened. "What have you learned?"

"They are cunning and resilient. They will be hard to dominate."

Darvus laughed aloud as he looked around at the fencing. "Yes, that is true."

Rezulin squatted. "The Humans offer much for knowledge of our technology."

"They wish us to become traitors, like you."

Rezulin flinched as if struck.

"Do we get to pick which Human we can eat? I choose the Fleet Admiral," Darvus said with a toothy smile.

Rezulin was silent. John hadn't discussed this with him, although he was pretty sure he wouldn't want to be eaten as part of the bargain. Maybe his mate, Jen, she never liked Rezulin.

"The choice is yours. Live like this," Rezulin pointed to the two lost Lizards seated in the edge of the compound, "till you slowly die or join the Humans."

Twenty minutes later, Darvus watched Rezulin exit the camp escorted by two marines.

John gazed at the lizards from the POW admin building. The long-range surveillance cameras zoomed in to record Darvus' every move in HD holo detail. He could almost hear the War Fleet Leader's brain cogs moving: 'What do the Humans really want by sending in Rezulin, the traitor?'

Chapter 8

Gnoll Frigate, *Wild Roar*

"I can't believe that insufferable furball Tyron. He stole that ship." Lord Saga's growl could be heard all the way to engineering. The five-ship raid on an Umphat convoy had been very successful despite Saga's complaints.

"What happened to you? When we attacked, you were right there on my port side," Lord Volund countered. The younger brother frowned at the area behind his sister. "That's not your bridge. Where are you?"

Saga moved closer to the screen.

"You're in engineering. Is something wrong?"

Saga rolled her eyes; her brother can be dense sometimes. She whispered, "You don't think I'd come to the bowels for nothing do you." Saga looked around at the heavy oxidation on the walls. It was engineering, after all. "The prima freighter fired an EMP missile at me and knocked my starboard engine.

"The lead freighter? You went for the most heavily armed freighter of the convoy on your own?" Volund laughed at his sister's recklessness. She was lucky to be alive.

Saga made to pout, then realized others in the room would see so changed it to a forced laugh.

"So, while I took all the fire, lord Tyron schmuck, hit their engines and took it as his prize."

Lord Volund's face stilled becoming serious. "Tyron claimed the prima."

Saga nodded.

The rivalry between the families was no secret. But taking another's kill was a serious breach of protocol. "The King will hear of this," he said.

Saga shuffled nervously.

Volund stared at her, "You claimed the ship and struck its hull, right?" Prey was only deemed a claimable kill if the hull is breached.

"Not exactly."

Volund stared intently at his sister. He knew she was desperate to raise her standing to be able to enter the house of lords. Doing so meant that she would be allowed into the King's hall, but to falsely claim a kill was almost as bad as stealing one.

"Brother, I fired missiles that might have breached, but my sensors failed with the EMP. Tyron could have only struck the engines if mine had damaged the vessel."

Volund said nothing.

"It was a whole rack of missiles," she said, her eyes grew moist and ears drooped. Gnoll rules of engagement were strictly adhered to. Deviating from them would shame the Pride in the eyes of the Gnoll aristocracy. Claiming a kill early short-circuits the distribution of prizes to the warriors. Prides live and die on their prizes. Normally the raid strategist assigns the kills, but he can be overturned by honorable claims.

Volund shut his eyes as he visualized the shame and said, "I'll deal with father."

"Really?" Saga's smile returned, she looked like a cub again despite her being the older of the two.

Volund smiled sadly and cut the connection.

Chapter 9

Gnoll Homeworld

"My daughter cub did this?" Lord Valerian was stunned.

The priest bowed and left the hall.

"Saga wouldn't," Saga's mother Cymbal declared.

"If this is true, our standing with the King is worse than I originally feared. Especially if the priest knows. No doubt the Sil'thik do as well."

Worry creased Cymbal's face. She knew she had taught Saga better than claiming a kill not hers. Especially when the convoy's route intel was provided by their Patron, the Sil'thik Insectoids. They would scrutinize all aspects of the raid with their own superior sensor technology. Nothing would lead back to them, as it could cascade into a Patron war.

The doors opened, and an attendant Ferret entered. "My Lord, Lord Volund bids entry."

Lord Valerian shuffled in his chair. They would find the truth of the allegations.

"Is he alone?" Lady Cymbal asked.

"Yes, my Lady."

Lady Cymbal stole a gaze at her mate Lord Valerian.

"Enter," Valerian forced out through gritted teeth.

Chapter 10

Squishy Island, Indian Ocean, Earth

John and Jen got the distinct impression that Drakmok, the Principal of Squishy Island, wasn't cut out to be a leader. Tela, on the other hand, understood the complexities of their problem immediately.

"So, what you're saying is that being a new spacefaring species we would be picked on by any and all comers from the Collective unless we had a protector, a Patron," Jen said.

"Yes. Unless you can demonstrate that you can protect yourselves," Tela added.

Jen looked over at John.

"But we beat the Lizards."

"That doesn't count, the Lizards ignore the Galactic Collective and vice versa unless they're eating them."

"By Galactic Collective, you mean the Patrons and Servant races excluding the Lizards?"

"Yes."

Jen squished her face in distaste.

"What if we showed them the battleship?" asked John.

"They would not believe you battled the lizards and won. Maybe you stole it? They would still attack you," Tela said. "You are unknown, new and small. In your first alien contact, you had only one world maybe two with a manufacturing base."

John laughed at the irony of it all. They had won, stolen and built so many warships including one they made themselves from a cargo container, but they were all discounted to nothing.

Tela and Drakmok shifted colors in their mantels to solid green::Curiosity::.

Jen frowned at the discoloration.

"The problem still remains, how do we join the Galactic Collective and not become some servant species?"

Tela's black eyes darted from one human to the other, then lingered on John, as if assessing his commitment.

"You must pick a fight and win."

John and Jen stared at the Squishy.

"Ok...?" *What the hell, pick a fight?*

"And not just any species. They have to be one with some standing, either a Patron or a high Servant race."

John frowned. "You're serious."

Tela nodded.

"Great, we can't just pick one of the wimps in school, we have to pick a fight with one of the bullies instead." They needed friends fast, to fight the Lizards, but only after picking a fight with their potential ally. John shook his head in dismay; this was nuts.

Tela and Drakmok looked at each other, then changed their mantle color to purple::confusion::.

Chapter 11

Caladan Moon Base, Titan

Mags was surprised when she received a 'you've got vid conference request' ping from Director Bill Withers, Chief of Security and head spook for the company. He was a well-built man, balding and in his late thirties to early forties when he appeared on her vid screen.

"Lt. Margaret Hanks?" Bill's corporate title showed up at the top of the screen.

"You're the Security Chief, shouldn't you already know?"

The man's face clearly showed he was initially taken aback, then he suddenly cracked a warm smile.

"Yes, you're quite right. I would like you to consider a proposition. I know that you signed on for the academic stream within the corporation. Something to do with Fauna-"

"Yes..." Mags was about to fill him in on the intricacies of biochemistry and biodiversity and such, but by the look the Director gave her, his call was not going to be a request.

"We need a security officer to babysit some scientists, present company excepted of course. They are going on a critical mission to Aries where you will be posted eventually. Unfortunately, the people we had lined up have been made unavailable."

Mags was about to speak up to deny that she had the training for the security officer role, but the Director gave her another look which shut her mouth.

"I know you feel undertrained, and this assignment is an important role. However, it is off world on a small new station we are setting up. Initially, there will only be six to a dozen people posted on the station. Your science background will assist the station Administrator with the decontamination module deployment."

"Unfortunately, of the twelve people going, one of those people must have some background in security. I noticed that you have certifications in quite a few of the basic requirements for security. I'll give the okay for you to get further training on the job where you can fill in the gaps in simulators on the station. This is not a long-term assignment."

Mags sat back, considering the man's request as she tussled her purple hair strands behind her left ear. "You say this posting is off-world, as in off-world in another star system?"

"Yes."

Another star system! She never thought that she would be included in such a project. Imagine! She may even be able to experience alien worlds firsthand for her studies. Plus being a security officer for a short while might be fun. She could then justifiably spend time on those harder physical courses she'd downloaded.

"Ok, I'll do it. When do I leave?"

"You should receive your orders within the next half hour. Be at dock 7H and report to Commander Ahmad no later than 1600 TST, on the 9th. Lieutenant make sure you are on time at the freighter's hatch because the *Kaluka* will not wait. Good luck, Hanks."

"Yes, sir." Mags cut the comm., she had a lot of packing to do; the 9th was in two days. She quickly brought up onscreen the certs she needed to pass for her Sec1, band3, security rating. She then checked it for equipment that she would need from stores: A Taser, an M48 carbine with Electro bullets and a set of flexible secure-cuffs. Smiling to herself, they could be interesting when she meets her next boyfriend.

Bill nodded and went about setting her user details up, her course authorizations, and security clearance for Rams Head. He looked at her bio once more; she'd lived a tough life and still come out with honors, so nodding his head he was confident she'd do well in the role.

Chapter 12

Squishy Isle. Indian Ocean

John and Jen walked into the conference room on Squishy Island. The sea salt smells permeated the soft coral covered walls and surroundings. Tela and Drakmok lay on the two wet spongey sofas. John had requested the two tell them more about the Galactic Collective, Patrons, and the older species.

Tela spoke of old wars between the Patrons where they had devastated star systems, killing intelligent species with every type of weapon, including dirty ones that irradiated planets. "These obscene practices did not stop the Patron wars. Some Patrons enhanced species, by modifying their Servant race's DNA with radiation tolerances, those irradiated worlds turned into manufacturing and business hubs because nothing else would survive. Certainly, nothing natural would grow."

"Eventually, the elder species came to an agreement at Tri Galfrey where they placed limits on weapon usage.

Much like your world has with nuclear fission and biological weapons of mass destruction."

Jen cleared her throat. "Is that where the Collective was created, where they formalized the relations between the Patrons and Servant species?"

Tela nodded, "At first, it was to stop destroying planets and other younger species. However, now I think they have it in place to stop new younger species from becoming Patrons. They all own Servant species; many of the weaker Servants would get crushed should there be a war between the Patrons.

"Any new species they discover get absorbed into their factions without a choice. They exploit all, including intelligent species, for their own selfish means. It's cheap for them, sentients are just another bioresource." Tela signaled with her tentacle to include the two humans, "We see it as slavery. To them, we are mere resources to be used or controlled."

"Phft," Jen hissed. "Sounds like a boss I know," Jen said, looking at John with a smile.

Tela looked to the two Humans and shifted her mantel color to green::curious::.

"Have there been any new Patrons at all since the Tri Gal... thingy accord started?" John asked, ignoring Jen's jibe.

"Yes, but not for a long time. The Veegans, they're a race of intelligent plants that use bee-like creatures to communicate, pollinating others with their views. They use generational ships to travel the stars. Their seed pods are astounding tech, everything you need for a new colony. I have never met them."

John sat back on the squelchy sofa, warm water dribbled down his legs.

"How do the lizards fit into this Galactic Collective?"

"They don't. There are a few species that just don't play well with others, the Lizards are one of them. The Carnivores and Scarabs don't either."

"Don't play well?" asked Jen.

"Because they eat sentients."

Jen's eyes owled as she shook her head.

"What will you do with all the lizard POWs?" Tela asked a little surprised they hadn't all been killed already. "They're dangerous."

John laughed. "You're telling me."

♦♦♦

Upon leaving Squishy Island, Jen brought up the latest news story hitting the international press, *alien rights.*

Mr. Lasiter had made a backflip on his attitude toward T.N., painting them in a favorable light. He wrote of his experience on other worlds.

He printed scathing articles on human morals and short-sighted government policies that highlighted the dangers of treating sentient species poorly in times of war. Abandoning mercy and compassion would be reciprocated by the enemy. Others pointed out in counter articles that the lizards eat people!', so all morals were off the dining table.

Chapter 13

The *Prize* - Lizard War Fleet, Sol System

The battle against the Lizard fleet within the solar system devastated the Terran Navy and other Earth Forces. The major spacefaring nations scrambled to grab as much alien technology from the derelict hulks in the battlespace as possible. Severe words were spoken in the UN against those aggressive countries using shuttles for tech salvage before the needs of the post-battle search and rescue operations.

John was uncompromising in his stance that T.N. took at least one of each type of lizard vessel into the T.N. fleet. It meant they got the battleship, the front half of a destroyer, one frigate and some smaller freighters that would augment their colony's supply chain once they were converted for Human use.

Before all the warships and support ships were distributed, scientists and troops from all over the Earth mobilized to protect their pending claims. Some even turning violent. There was a constant stream of shuttles and freighters from Earth's surface to the prize Lizard fleet. Space salvage became the new buzz word. The ships trundled like a trail of ants to a pile of sugar cubes.

A new exclusion zone was set up preventing any of the derelicts from being brought into Earth's orbit. Many on earth were wary of *accidental* orbital bombardment.

The hive of activity brought about a general expectation of massive technological development. Space industry start-ups and stocks skyrocketed.

Midship Airlock 4, Lizard Battleship *Shesha*

It had been four weeks since the last Human survivor of the battle for Earth had been rescued. Slow governmental debates continued to equivocate the number of dollars that should be expended to rescue any remaining Lizards still trapped on the derelict ships.

Meanwhile, despite the international debate, T.N. continued to retrieve the remaining lizards within the space debris and transfer them to their POW camp in W.A.

"Sergeant has the boat been cleared?" the Lieutenant said to the armored space marine. They were tasked with clearing the last lizards from the battleship *Shesha*.

"Yes, sir. Got the last cold blood squared away on the shuttle."

"Very well. Leave a squad here to protect the scientists in case there's a straggler still on board."

"Yes, sir."

A small team of T.N. scientists and engineers assigned to assess the battleship *Shesha* walked around the massive bridge. They were given the task of evaluating the tech from a scaled-up perspective. Humans could build small ships like a frigate, but the challenges of building a behemoth would be very different. The group was amazed at the tech from their first moments aboard the vessel. They were confronted with oddities such as the interior walls that constantly morphed from shape to shape, building corridors seemingly at random. Each non-descript wall looked like any other making navigating through them extremely difficult. The wall surface was dry yet slippery to the touch like silk. Below its Teflon like exterior was surprisingly warm. These properties made deep analysis problematic because the walls seem to exhibit virtual signs of life. The human sensors were made to measure non-living things.

"How do they tell where to go in this maze?" Cal said.

Dr. Joy Sneddon examined the soft, warm surface then sneezed. "They use scent."

"What?"

"Well, this wall smells different to that one."

"You mean they smell their way around the ship?"

"Ah, huh. They may even lick it with their tongues," she said distractedly. Dr. Joy had moved on.

"Joy, have you ever seen this stuff before?" Cal stood before the massive screen and pointed to the Lizard Poetry that scrolled down the main viewscreen on the bridge. The characters formed interesting patterns on the monochrome screen. Cal understood basic Akio Lizard dialect. However, the script seemed to be an archaic form of it and nearly impossible to read.

"No, amazing, huh? It's says something about Scarabs and victory, I think. I guess this ship fought against the Scarabs at different star systems, including one called Gil'latrek, wherever that is."

Suddenly, all power within the battleship wound down and died. The only exception was the green message in the archaic Akio Lizard script flashing on the war leader's console. Lights flickered then flashed a warning before they turned off completely. Physical access to the main fusion reactors was unceremoniously cut as bulkheads closed on each of the reactors surprising the stunned engineers.

"Oh my God," Joy cried out in alarm as she staggered around in the semi-darkness waiting for her eyesight to return. The boarding party scrambling to turn on their suit lights. "We just lost all power!" Joy yelped as the gravity plating also disengaged.

The bland walls turned a light shade of blood red.

All through the fleet, scared Humans repeated the same curses as each of the Lizard vessels shut down. Their first thoughts were of being left stranded, it hadn't occurred to them yet that without power to regulate air and heat, the prize ships could quite easily become their tombs.

T.N. Space Command Center, Titan

The full implication of what was happening within the prize fleet didn't strike Earth's leadership until the breathless chattering cries of alarm from their boarding parties echoed through the comm channels. The commandeered Lizard ships were having power shutdowns that cutoff life support, which meant those aboard would suffer a slow, dark death by freezing or asphyxiation through carbon monoxide poisoning.

Commander Beckett contacted Jason when the comm chatter suddenly exploded with requests for help.

"Admiral, we are getting reports of reactor shutdowns across the prize fleet."

"What? Why the hell would they shut down?"

The officers around him stared back blankly.

Jason shook himself to action. "Scramble the SAR teams and get them over there quickly," he ordered his staff. Jason turned his comm to Titan Teleport Control, where the Duty Captain responded. "How many groups do we have a fix on that we can transport out?"

"Even if we could transport a SAR team to each individual ship, the loss of power means that each closed room is potentially a death trap. How could they open the door when there is no power? Transporting them out instead is just as problematic, accurate targeting of people without a transponder is risky," the captain said.

Jason turned to his comm officer, "Get one of those damn Lizards on the phone and find out what's going on with these ships! Commander, make sure you advise Fleet Admiral Stevenson and the UN liaison."

Jason switched tack to his adjutant. "I want the maintenance areas of Titan, Ceres and Dragon Trees to scrounge up every single laser, blowtorch or door opener they can get within the next 15 minutes. Oh, don't forget the space stations."

Switching channels to space traffic control (Titan STC), Jason went on. "Lieutenant, I want you to contact every single ship we have out there that is potentially able to dock with the Lizard fleet giving them air and life-support."

"Admiral, Colonel Manders is on the comm."

Jason switched channels on his comm. "Eric, we got a huge snafu here. The prize fleet has gone dark. We need SAR teams deployed on them now because we've got close to twenty Lizard ships with still air and no power. In three or four hours without a suit, they'll die from exposure."

"Ok Jason, I'll contact Major Bridges from Dragon Trees Garrison to coordinate SAR teams from Earth, if you can get them transported to the stricken ships. I'll personally command the Ceres and Titan SAR teams from here."

Lt. Hiro from Comms spoke out. "Admiral, Fleet Admiral Stevenson is on the comm."

"John, we have a situation here. The Lizard fleet has gone dark. We have thousands of scientists, engineers and soldiers on board, not to mention Earth Forces. Can you get some sense out of the Lizards there, we need to know our options '*pronto.*'"

"Shit, okay, I'll talk to Darvus."

◆◆◆

Brindella Lizard POW Camp, Western Australia

After a quick flight on the *Grace* to Western Australia, John, Rezulin, and the four marines that trailed behind him strode into the POW compound. His face was grim as they made directly for Darvus.

John was taken by surprise at the shocking condition of some of the Lizards that shuffled slowly through the camp. Their vacant looks matched their lifeless discolored scales. They moved mechanically without spacial awareness dragging their tails through the mud and dirt behind them. John realized he needed to chase up Fiona and the med reports for the POWs. But for now, he felt his anger fuel his body. He needed some answers, and Darvus was the oracle.

"Why have the Lizard ships shut down?" John demanded of the Fleet War Leader when he arrived. He had a pretty good idea but wanted Darvus to respond, setting the tone of the interview. John asked questions, Darvus answered them.

Darvus stared at John for a long moment. "All of our ships have an auto shutdown. This progressively disables the ship if security codes are not entered into the vessel's computer. There are only a few officers from each ship that know those codes." Darvus was quiet about the shutdown process.

"Shit." John cursed. Turning aside, John tapped his com. "Jason, there's a dead man switch in each of the ships with a passcode. Just like the Godzilla."

"What, a self-destruct? So, air and heat are not the only problems."

"No. How many Lizards are left in the debris?"

Darvus flinched. "You have not gotten all the Lizards crews out yet? But it's been weeks!"

John turned back toward the two lizards and shrugged.

"We just need to reenter the codes," said Darvus coolly.

John stared back at the Fleet War Leader then at Rezulin who didn't look too surprised. "Those same code you said were old and wouldn't work?"

Darvus blew air through his teeth, then nodded.

John ground his teeth. "I see," he said then scrutinized the War Leader. Was that a sign of smugness in the lizard's blinking? Over the weeks the Fleet War Leader had seemed nervous. But now... Was the damn second inner eyelid a sign? The lizard's head and shoulders were relaxed, and he seemed relieved, even calm. Had Darvus been comforted by the possibility that Humans would get stuck within the Lizard ships when the power failed?

John had suspected the switches were there because of the Godzilla's self-destruct. He had hoped Darvus would be forthcoming on his own. And yet John was a little surprised that Darvus showed some empathy toward his trapped crews, and not just written them off. He couldn't fault the lizards for the self-destructs, because he had done the same thing to the jump drives on all the Human ships as insurance if anyone tried to steal the tech. Would he blow them knowing humans were aboard? He didn't want to think about it. He hoped he wouldn't be able to, but this was war... people died in all sorts of ways.

Darvus had never been forthcoming with their tech. John gritted his teeth, feeling the tense anger wash over him despite it being hypocritical.

"Did Rezulin fully explain the offer of what we call political asylum to you? *The asylum was conditional on your co-operation.* That would include handing over the ship codes. If Humans die because of the shutdown, it will become politically impossible to give you asylum. You must decide now."

Darvus looked at John then pointed to Rezulin. "He mentioned that Humans don't kill their captives, nor do they enslave them... ?"

"Yes, that's true, and?" John asked.

"What else is there? We will return to the Empire without honor. The Empire will make use of us as slaves or food." Darvus' tail slumped, he seemed resigned.

"No," John shook his head, "you stay here and work with us."

"How are we not slaves if we work for you?"

"Do you wish to return to the Empire? ... Well?"

"No," Darvus said, his second eyelid shutting.

John had planned to provide a haven for the Lizard war veterans with the resources of a colony and some self-determination. In return, the new Lizard community would help defend all Human worlds. He explained it once more to the big lizard.

"We would be reborn Human... do we get to eat Humans?"

John flinched. "No, no eating sentients."

"Not even dead ones?"

"No!"

"You condemn us to a fixed state of our current DNA."

"No, you can alter your DNA, but without eating others."

Darvus turned to stare at Rezulin, and John knew Darvus thought the Humans were hypocrites. John ground his back teeth to stop from screaming out *'Pete, please forgive me! I didn't realize what it would mean!'* John clamped down hard with his jaw straining it.

"Very well, we will not eat sentient brains," Darvus compromised. "We get our own world?"

"Not exactly, there will be other species there, including Humans."

Rezulin and Darvus both looked to John at this new twist.

"As equals." John continued.

Darvus contemplated the offer as he sized up John. "I will consult the other War Leaders."

John looked at Rezulin. "Lord Darvus cannot decide for all. He is no longer Fleet War Leader and cannot command them," Rezulin said in explanation.

John watched Darvus shuffle away toward a clump of Lizards talking amongst themselves, his tail snaked back and forth as if chastened. Rezulin sat on the dirt and pointed to the ground at John's feet.

"It will take time," was all Rezulin said.

John sat and stared at the group of motley Lizards near the walls. They looked sick with their skin dry and drawn despite the ample fountains around the camp. Their mouths hung open with drool.

Darvus had a headache. Humans were more confusing than he ever believed possible. *Not enslaved, but working for them? How is that different to slavery? They would give his crew a new world...? What did he mean by 'equals,' is it some weird Human ritual concept?*

Darvus shook his head to clear his thoughts. What mattered was they get a new world with self-determination, assuming the Fleet Admiral was good for his word. *What was he to do now? Giving the Humans the codes to the computers would ultimately give them their warship technology.* How patriotic could he afford to be given that on his return to the Empire, *if* he returned, he and the crew would all be killed out-of-hand?

Allying with these Humans would be an unholy alliance. Darvus smiled as if a weight lifted from his shoulders, Fleet War Leader, ha! There was no fleet now. He had no right to order other Lizards to do his bidding. They would need to make up their own mind, just as he did when deciding to take up John's offer versus staying a patriot to return as a prisoner marked for death.

Darvus looked at each of the faces around him. Many he had worked with for years, on different campaigns. "What is your decision?"

As each War Leader gave their response, he felt guilty that his decision would influence theirs, to join him in the unholy alliance. War Leader Sarrin snarled at Darvus with silent words of traitor written on his muzzle.

Darvus was dismayed that so many War Leaders decided to remain loyal to the Empire. They and their crews would die.

The Fleet War Leader shuffled toward where John and Rezulin sat. His slow tail swing and gait seemed old and tired. "I will give you the reactivation security codes to the *Shesha*."

Almost half of the group of leaders, those that had voted to remain loyal, walked further into the POW camp. Darvus turned his head toward them, "Do not hold your hopes high for those leaders that remain in the camp."

Chapter 14

The Now Derelict Lizard Fleet

The Lizard battleship *Shesha* cast an evil spell over those that closed in on her. A joyless, somber atmosphere gripped the passengers and crew of the *Grace* as they approached the lizard warship. John pushed forward on the helm control sweeping the *Grace* around behind the jutting guns, and spherical comms antenna array. Away from the Sun, they entered the shadowy dark side, and a large area of the heavens was blackened by the hull's bulky silhouette. Small blinking lights outlined the port hangar bay, a small refuge from the pitch black. The darkness and alien origin filled John with a sense of foreboding. The ship was all but dead in space. He was there to reinitialize the security codes and save the twenty-two personnel currently aboard that were stranded.

John felt his skin crawl as he flew the *Grace* into the jaws of the beast. The fight for Earth was still vivid in his mind, including the hard-fought boarding action he'd seen vicariously through the marine boarding party head cams. The fierce fighting to take the lizard battleship was not something one could forget. Without further prompting, the faces of those who had fought and died in that action cascaded through John's mind.

Jen leaned over and snapped on the external lights, giving them all a reprieve from the oppressive blanket surrounding the ship.

"Max, set Channel 5," John said to the wiry Geek sitting at his console.

"Are you ready?" John asked Jen as she floated toward the rear cargo area. Max acknowledged the channel change and glanced at his wristwatch; it was five in the morning on Titan, where he had been based the last two weeks. They had been working the search and rescue all night. He could barely stifle the yawn that tried to escape his lips.

"Did she keep you up all night?" Jen asked with a cheeky smile.

"If you call programming orbital mechanics into the Astro Devils a 'she,' well then yep." Although the small, nimble ships could dogfight in close range space, optimizing orbital mechanics for long-range targets made a huge impact on their fuel and life support needs.

Chemical thrusters were included as a backup in case the normal electric ion engines failed because of an EMP.

Jen shook her head at the insanity of some IT geeks.

"Just don't fall asleep when we're inside," John said in a mock authoritarian tone.

"I got that covered," Max said as he flipped the lid of a pill bottle spilling the little white capsules in 20 different directions due to the zero gravity. Max unclipped his seat belt and dived open-mouthed at the nearest floating stim.

Jen shook her head and danced around the remaining floating tablets making her way to the bridge hatch control.

John frowned at Max's use of stimulants. Without saying another word, he floated through the now open hatch then on to the cargo area where the rest of the SAR team was preparing to disembark.

John and Jen led the SAR team using the security access code given to them by Darvus. Lizard warships were made of clusters of concentric egg-shaped modules within an outer shell. Each cluster brought them closer to high-value operations or machinery. Hatches within the ship opened in different ways giving the crew access. Jen had a working theory that the different lizard body types defined their preferences for entry. They thanked their lucky stars that the entry code had been accepted by every hatch so far, much like the admin password on a computer system.

"Try again," the squad leader said to Private Mousy, the 300-pound musclebound Mr. Universe marine. The beefcake looked comical, hunched over the small data pad by the door.

"I'm telling you, it's not working."

"Admiral, it looks like our free pass just expired."

John sighed. He knew it was too good to be true. They still had a dozen compartments to get through to the bridge. The code needed to be entered into the Fleet War Leader's console for it to unlock the whole ship.

"Where's the breach that Col. Manders used to get to the bridge?"

"Sir, if we backtrack to this junction, then make a right. Through two doors, we'll then match up with his entry point."

John nodded. "Okay, let's get to it." Each keyed entry had turned on the lights as they proceeded. That wouldn't be the case once they followed Col. Manders route.

John tapped his comm while he looked at Jen. "Max, we've had a block, our key card is no longer effective. We will be tracing Eric's route to the bridge."

"Understood. Aaah, Admiral Dunn has been attempting to find you."

"Mmm, I'm using the 3rd rule of Max," John said aloud.

Jen squished her face in confusion.

"It's best to ask forgiveness..."

Jen and John could hear Max. "Pfft! That doesn't always work."

Jen laughed. "He's miffed that you caught on to his antics."

John shrugged and pulled out his PDA to check the little device was wirelessly linked to *Grace's* shipnet. Using Col. Mander's original boarding party's ship plan they had on file was useless. The walls had since reconfigured like a maze that changed. John had heard whispers of this phenomenon from some of the investigative teams. However, he assumed it was just over-excited imaginations on the part of the reporting scientist. Now he knew better, and it was damn inconvenient.

It took Jen's lateral thinking to use the *Grace* and other nearby vessels as a compass to get around the problem. It took longer than they expected, but at least they were moving in the right direction.

On the datapad was a representation of the battleship. Within the wireframe, it was infested with flashing icons and the last known location of the distressed humans.

John wondered whether the extra compressed air pack he had added to his regular supply was going to be enough. The ship was enormous.

John turned to watch Jen carefully step between the jagged edges of the hatch where Midshipman Janus had cut through it with her new breaching hot plasma torch.

Janus pulled the fourth plasma chemical cartridge from her pack. The unit was a variation on a breaching tool used by the US military on Earth. She was getting used to positioning the torch against the alien doors. Checking everyone was at a safe distance, "fire in the hole, fire in the hole, fire in the hole," she yelled out before tugging on the cartridge loop. Unlike the previous doors, this seemed weaker, so Janus quickly moved the torch around the edges tracing out a door frame. Bright plasma spat out of the end of the torch, liquefying the metal as she moved it.

Sudden explosive decompression ripped through the partially liquid door dragging Janus half through its melting breach.

Janus screamed. "Damn shiiit!!!" as her suit arm melted into shreds. Jets of plasma blew out from the torch as it flew through zero-G buffeted by the ship and her suit decompressing. Private Mousy screamed when the torch spiraled toward the big man.

The weakened hatch ripped the remainder of the door from its housing, taking Janus and her mutilated arm with it. The sudden drop in pressure struck the remaining SAR team knocking them from their magnetized boots. Two SAR members smacked into Mousy from behind while caught in the wind tunnel. Stumbling forward Mousy let out a hysterical high-pitched toddler's scream, that crossed the radio channel.

Loose materials, lights, and air tanks flew through the massive hole striking Janus who was flailing on the deck with her right arm caught in the wrecked door under her.

The precious ship's air whisked out through holes sustained in the battle for Earth where they were breached. Eric had used the breach tactic to clear some of the lizards in the cleanup. Light curtains kept the air leakage under control. However, with the reactors on standby, the curtains had disengaged to save power.

Slowly the team extricated the now unconscious Janus and assigned her one of the SAR members to get her back to the *Grace*. Her lower right arm was missing; it was burnt to a cinder.

"Mousy, shut up." The reprimand from the SAR team lead was enough to stop the big man in his tracks.

The next two hatches were boring in comparison. Private Ahman took over from Janus. Unfortunately, his technique was somewhat lacking compared to the midshipman. He would often leave jagged edges surrounding the mount.

Gritting his teeth, John hated to see Jen risking her life. Even the slightest rip to a skin suit could be fatal.

"This can't be right, we've been through here!" Mousy cried out across the live channel.

"Settle down, Mousy," said Darcy, his squad leader.

"I got no air!" Mousy complained the third time.

"You got plenty, I just checked your stats."

"No, I got no air," he screamed. Mousy's voice jumped two octaves. Suddenly the big man was hitting his helmet with his gloved fist.

"Stop trying to break your helmet," he said as he bumped into Mousy from behind.

Mousy took a deep breath and screamed. His big hands flailed as he pushed off away from Darcy.

Bounding down the hallway towards John and Jen, was a 300-pound flying balloon. Yes, the man was weightless, but the impact was still based on a 300-pound man flying along the corridor like a freight train.

Mousy's eyes were bulging as his mouth gasped for oxygen.

"Stop! You're hyperventilating," Mousy's team leader yelled through the comm.

A quick turn of his head didn't prevent the man from smashing into the ceiling with such force that would have killed an ordinary person. Blood spurted from Mousy's nose where he had hit an internal frame in his helmet.

The crazed man flew down the corridor like a juggernaut, directly toward John, Jen and escape.

John turned to Jen, who was straddled over the last makeshift door entrance. "Quickly, get out of there!" Jen had a leg in each sector. If Mousy plowed into her, there was no doubt her leg, and her suit would be severely damaged.

Mousy gulped, causing more blood to fly from his nose. The Zero-G made the blobs splatter his face and inside helmet alarming him further. Although there was no difference swallowing in zero gravity, his hyped-up panic attack was making him choke on the small amount of blood there was.

Several squaddies scrambled down the corridor after him to bring the horse of a man under control. But the dark and the Zero-G strengthened Mousy's resolve to avoid capture.

Jen lifted her boot to step through into John's corridor, but the magneto within its sole flashed on, snagging part of the jagged door with its magnetism. Her momentum forward tripped her and twisting her onto her back to swing horizontally 2 feet off the ground flailing her arms in the Zero G. Without a surface to push against, she was stuck like a turtle on its back.

Mousy rolled over, cartwheeling his way past John heading directly towards Jen and the deadly metallic edge.

"Shit," John yelped. In slow, deliberate movements, he aligned his legs and feet, pushing off like a missile towards Jen. It was a race between John and the panic-stricken Mousy.

John sped after Mousy in the Zero G. He had never been inspired to try out for the football team when he was growing up. He regretted it now as he forced himself to focus.

"Mousy, dammit!"

The marine was like a charging rhinoceros, oblivious to his surroundings.

John could see Jen frantically trying to reach the deck to push off and try to detangle herself.

Mousy bounced against the side of the corridor and kept on going.

John stretched out and tapped Mousy's boot as he dived for the man's legs. The man spun in Zero-G, slamming his head against the ceiling once again to careen into the bulkhead just above Jen. They all heard through the comm the sickening crunch his body made as it struck.

Jen looked up at the heavyset man and hoped that gravity didn't re-engage at that second.

"Stay put, Private!" John said, pointing up at Mousy on the ceiling. To John's relief, the dazed man did as he was told.

"I'm getting too old for this shit."

Buoyed by his tap tackle, John bounced towards Jen in an easy bound. Despite all the recent tragedy, John fronted Jen with a relieved smile.

John helped Jen snap her mag boots to the deck just as Mousy's immediate superior arrived. "Well, shit, Mousy, you could have killed the Commander. Get your dumb ass over in dog position where I can keep an eye on you," the team leader commanded as he bounced up to the ceiling to check on the 300 pound private. Despite the health status bars on his HUD, he wanted to physically check Mousy in case the readings were wrong.

The SAR team leader switched to a private channel with the Admiral. "I'm sorry for Mousy nearly braining the Commander sir."

John was still breathing heavily. "Do what you need to get us all back safe Lieutenant. That includes Mousy."

"Yes, sir."

The group moved carefully on through the last remaining corridors to the bridge. John walked around bridge taking in the myriad of manual consoles and antiquated looking computer systems giving it a steampunk feel. On a human ship, many of the spaceship functions would assign to a computer. However, this was not the case on a lizard warship, important functions were given to specialized lizards to perform the task. John shook his head at the astro-navigation station. A lizard with a large brain and massive calculating capacity would sit there making the subspace Alcubierre bubble calculations. Those complex calculations allowed a ship to enter subspace without being torn to pieces. Astonishingly, they were all done in their heads.

John moved to the Fleet Admiral's console. The three tired structure allowed the Admiral to see all the sections from his pedestal. Pressing a blue button, then a ten alien digit code. John checked twice that the code he entered was correct. Not only the characters were different, but they were using a base 12 numbering system. Once he had entered the security codes into the bridge console, full power and operations were restored.

The SAR on the battleship ran relatively smoothly after that except when Jason caught up with the recalcitrant command team members. John even managed to seem contrite, much to Max's surprise.

Chapter 15

The Now Derelict Lizard Fleet

John and Jason sat crowded in front of the laptop WebCam. Their hushed tones and short, precise responses portrayed a seriousness to the issue at hand. The screen was filled with Eric's confident yet angry face as he reported on the progress of the search and rescue (SAR) operations carried out on personnel within the Lizard warships.

"Twelve ships still have inspection teams stranded on board. The rest of the ships were badly damaged or had not yet had an assessment." Some of the vessels were far off in the Kuiper belt. Just getting there took time. "Seven of those ships were claimed by Earth Forces, and we've sent what codes we had for those ships to their liaisons. The Indians and the British have requested SAR assistance."

On the sensor viewscreen, the signal for one of the lizard frigates reactor's disappeared, leaving electromagnetic traces of an explosion. "Shit," Eric exclaimed, his face dark.

"Did we have people onboard?" John asked.

Eric scanned his HUD listings. "Phil's team were assigned to that ship." Turning away, he spoke off-screen.

His face was somber when he returned. "He had a squad of five with him." There was an awkward silence. "Of the five ships claimed by T.N., we have only two command codes. One is the battleship *Shesha* that you reinitialized."

Eric continued, "The freighter is a different story, we're unsure why the codes have not been successful. However, the engineers are working on it. The destroyer we claimed has no poetry on board and no code request."

Jason snorted. It was probably because the back half of the ship was crushed, which included the main reactors. It was a miracle that the ship didn't blow during the battle. They would have to add a backend and replace the fusion plant before she'd move again if she ever did. She's pretty banged up.

"Eric, if they can't resolve either ship startup within an hour, I want the teams off the ships. They can try again, well after the self-destruct timer deadline has run out," said John as he stared intently into the screen.

"Saving tech is good, but what about personnel?"

"All the jump drives within the Sol system are being utilized to either extract personnel or pump warm air into the affected areas of the ships until we can get to them. Several of the ships are on a slow ballistic course that could cause a problem if they're not redirected. I've asked Jen to look into that, and if necessary, tow the ships to safety."

"Are we certain that we have a full listing of all personnel that was working or assigned to the Lizard warships?" John asked.

"As far as T.N. personnel are concerned, we are fairly certain that we have everyone accounted for. However, regarding Earth Forces, the governments are a little cagey about who they've sent and where they've sent them."

"Very well, do what you can, Eric," John replied with a sigh, sharing his dismay at the callousness of the governments involved.

"What of the Lizards? Are there any still on ships that we know of? Are there any ships we haven't yet swept for survivors?" John knew they were basically covered; otherwise, he wouldn't have gone for the battleship so readily.

Eric looked off to the side for confirmation. "No. We picked them all up and transported them to Bindella POW. The last was picked up with the Belgians on the EU Earth Forces claim."

By the end of the week, it was surprising that so few people had died within the derelict hulks. Half of the hulls exploded within days of the first scuttled spaceship. There was some backlash from the lack of SAR coordination but more importantly, from the lack of POW Lizard cooperation. There were many reasons why the cooperative Lizards did not inform the Human liaison of the security shutdown.

Darvus was cooperative, after the fact, when the ships started to shut down. John was furious with his silence. This political disaster was going to make it even more difficult to handle, especially given the Lizards were going to be relocated on one of the new colony worlds in the Harmony system, ahead of many Humans who desired to move there.

◆◆◆

Brindella Lizard POW Camp, WA.

Two weeks after the Lizard prize fleet was deemed safe, the *Grace* and three shuttles from the freighter *Aneska* dropped down through the atmosphere and landed at the entrance to the main POW camp in Western Australia.

John entered the camp to a sea of deep-set alien eyes. Many Lizards had seen the shuttle's arrival and anticipated a long trip to a dirty slave mining planet, despite the assurances made by the humans. At least they wouldn't be stuck in the camp.

"Darvus," John greeted the Lizard War Leader as the seven-foot lizard gracefully dipped his head in respect. "The *Aneska* will take you to Cresseda, a Human colony where you will be able to make a new life." John couldn't read the Lizard. He suspected the Lizard didn't believe him.

"The Human leader there is Governor Willoughby. You will liaise with him for resources. Housing and lizard foods have already been stockpiled for your use."

Darvus nodded slowly.

John turned to a commotion at the camp exit gates between T.N. guards and two aggravated Lizards. Shuttle engines idled just outside the fence but couldn't hide the angry retorts.

John walked over to the ruckus, "What's going on here?" he said, using his command voice.

The two marines on guard duty turned to John and straightened. "Admiral, these two Lizards were attempting to leave but have not signed the Political Asylum Agreement." The first Marine held up his weapon, keeping it trained on the two cold-bloods.

John walked over to the two Lizards with Darvus trailing. "What is your name and designation?"

The two Lizards turned to John, claws clenched, but said nothing.

A second Marine brought his weapon up to aim at the Lizards.

Darvus stepped forward around John and made a lightning move that struck the first Lizard heavily in the jaw. "You will return to the enclosure."

Blood seeped around the Lizard's teeth giving him a savage Jurassic look. Maintaining eye contact, the two rebel Lizards walked defiantly back within the enclosure, shoulders back and their tails high.

"Do not release them," Darvus said. "Silar and Hemmel will not honor the peace accord."

Despite the altercation, John was heartened by Darvus' response.

John turned around, seeking a large man with stripes on his armored breastplate and cuff. "I have assigned Senior Sergeant Johnson as your aide for Human affairs."

Once again, Darvus dipped his head.

"Good luck," John said as he held out his hand. Darvus looked at it, then held his out as well, without touching.

John smiled, nodded, and walked away, back towards the *Grace*. "Meet you next in Cresseda."

Chapter 16

Alpha Artetis System (Rams Head Station?)

Grace's engines idled as she sat in a geosynchronous orbit over the only gas planet in the system. John, Max, and Jen took in the majesty of the turbulent swirling atmosphere far below them. Unlike other gas giants, this one was ringed with crystalline shards of reflective carbon and hydrogen with some as crystalline methane. The shards reflected the sunlight to create a beautiful but deadly rainbow halo effect in the upper atmosphere and beyond.

John could imagine any ship attempting to land on the planet would be ripped to shreds by diamond crystal shards flying at supersonic speeds.

Six months earlier, an automated probe was sent here to deploy an astrogation beacon and gain intelligence on the star system. The system was in the direction of a known trader run system run by Ferrets. The astrogation chart taken from the Squishy ship the *Kator* had it listed as a deadly station but *'Incredible for the sale of farm machinery, personal weapons, and wine trading. Warning, locals eat Squishy appendages as a delicacy. Astro node 766.987.112 Comm frequency 1187Tc.'* The chart was one of the few that were successfully retrieved before the Squishys destroyed the rest in a frenzy to prevent revealing the location of their new Homeworld.

"Are we receiving the probe telemetry?"

"5 by 5. Scan downloads are in progress."

John nodded. The scans should show if there were any visitors since the probe was teleported here.

Jen swiped her holo control, a 3D map of the system flickered to life on the console between her and John. The image slowly turned, giving a better idea of the celestial bodies in the system.

John had sent a probe from Earth to the Arietis System because it was a quarter of the distance from Earth to the trader system. John concentrated on the holo. The probe reported that the system contained a single star several times brighter than Sol's sun and a gas giant double the size of Jupiter. Twelve smaller lifeless moons surrounded the gas giant and danced in a complex pattern of orbital mechanics. There was a mixed expanse of asteroids and protoplanets that circled the star. John wondered what could have happened in the system to eliminate all heavy (dense) planets.

The System had nothing of major interest in it. It would be perfect, nothing of interest, meant fewer if any visitors.

Jen got out of her seat and floated her way to the nearby cabin quarters.

A muffled "Damn," came through the open hatch. Jen could usually cuss with the best of them.

"Jen, you ok?" John looked over as she reappeared with a scrunched nose.

"Yeah, but the shower is stuffed. The water reclamation machine must have something wrong with the filters." John could hear Jen unclip the unit to see the cartridge. "Eeew, there's slime all through it. That's what's making the smell."

"I'll go get another," John said climbing out of the helm seat. "Crap," he said a few minutes later as he came back from the stores cupboard. "The two in there have spoiled. There was a leak from the hull quick auto-seal packet." They would need to ensure in the future that they were stored separately.

Jen held the offending filter at arms-length as she rushed for the trash compactor.

John pulled out his pad that was connected to the shipnet and flicked through the stores menu, he flagged it for restocking.

John then switched to access the water levels. They had water, but he wanted to keep a large margin for emergency oxygen. They could generate O2 with pure water, however now that the water couldn't be recycled, he decided that they couldn't use any more H2O for bathing or other non-essentials.

Jen looked at John and pursed her lips; it would get stinky in here. The water filter might not be the worst of the smell by the time they got back.

♦♦♦

It took the *Grace* another two days to analyze and make a detailed map of the system. Two days without a shower because *Grace's* recycling was playing up, the cabin smelled ripe. John refused to return to civilization knowing he would not get back here any time soon.

Jen could smell the two men from her console. She scrunched her nose. "Yep, the system has one J class gas giant, and a whole bunch of asteroids," Jen sniped. She and John had fought over them taking such risks as exploring new star systems when they had a whole division of qualified people to do it for them. John had worked on her for days and eventually convinced her that they needed a break, and an exciting, adventurous holiday that could also fill in some gaps in his plan. They needed forward bases that could give them spheres of influence over the surrounding star systems.

"Look, we couldn't ask for a better system. There are resources here, but no planets that would be worth terraforming to entice other species to stay within it."

Jen looked at John and scowled. "No crisp mountain stream bathing water either, just Troll Mountain."

"Max, can you turn on the message buoy tach-com and send a message back to Titan fleet ops. Tell them they have a green light to teleport the space station and the *Versailles* here."

Fifteen minutes later a small message buoy disappeared from the Grace's cargo space on its way toward Sol. Since the battle for Earth, there had been discovered some teleporter accidents that could only be attributed to the aftermath of the battle and the high-pressure porting during the SAR operation from the derelicts. Constant porting had created deadly zones within the battle sphere that had warped space like a pretzel. A small team had been set up to investigate it and map the *no-teleport zones.*

In the meantime, teleporting cargo within the solar system had been restricted to small masses or snail freighter. This meant that the space station to be sent to

Rams Head would be an earlier model designed around mass restrictions.

No pretzel zones had been found outside of the solar system. So, traveling to the edge of the system's gravity well would avoid any problem areas. The only wrinkle was that the Frigate would arrive before the space station. Both were to be transported near *Grace's* position in the Rams Head system.

T.N. Versailles, Caladan Shipyard, Titan

Captain Josephine la Perouse was unsure how to respond to the latest orders she'd received. She was to be sent with her ship to a distant system that was, so far as she knew, lifeless, based on the data sent back by a probe six months ago. Why send a ship to a star system with nothing in it? Although this was a good opportunity to study celestial phenomena around a totally new star, she felt put out as her ship had only just returned to active service. All jump capable ships including hers were being upgraded with the security changes where the jump drive transporter and gravity projectors had explosives set in its casing to prevent tampering or reverse engineering. It was a top-secret maintenance directive that had stranded her in Titan's shipyard for the better part of a week. The bombs didn't make her feel comfy and cozy at night, having a dozen of those things all around the ship. She was wondering how long it would be before the crew found out and protested. A legitimate protest, in her eyes.

Josephine looked over at her XO; they had both been bemused by the orders assigning them to Rams Head System. She wondered if the orders were a vindictive payback for her father's actions or if T.N. bureaucracy was so out of control with the inefficiencies of one hand not knowing what the other was doing. There weren't many jump capable ships available in-system to protect Earth and yet, here she was being sent off to nowhere land where there was nothing but a giant gas planet, some protoplanets and a large asteroid field. Where's the sense in that?

She shook her head once more at the idiocy. When she'd questioned her orders, Admiral Dunn had shut her down, telling her to get with the program and follow damn orders. Straightening her tunic, she sat straight in her command chair. From her elevated position, she scanned her bridge for any alerts. All sections had reported green for launch.

"XO, are we ready to cast off?" the old-fashioned term for launching vessels from space-dock was still used by many of the European naval officers.

"All Section Chiefs report ready for departure. Stores loaded and secure, TTC has given permission to cast off, Captain."

The Captain took one last look around the bridge then nodded to the comm officer who pressed the ship-wide comm. "All hands, prepare for undocking, three-minute warning." Subdued klaxons echoed throughout the ship, warning of the pending ship movements.

The XO looked at his watch as a timer flicked up on the main viewer.

After three minutes, the XO nodded to the Operations officer who worked on his control board.

"Comms, notify TTC of cast-off." The comms officer spoke quietly into her headset.

"Secure all hands," echoed throughout the ship.

Airlocks sealed automatically, the outside hatch closed and clunked with finality.

"Airlock closed and sealed. The gangway has retracted."

"Decouple the umbilical," the Captain said to her XO.

"Umbilical has disengaged. Ship's Environment, reports green across the board, Captain."

"Disengage locking clamps."

Capt. La Perouse could feel the vibration caused by the magnetized docking clamps disengaging.

The XO turned to the helm. "Helm, take us out, slow and steady."

"Yes, sir."

Small lights lit warnings that displayed on the main viewer as electric thrusters jockeyed the ship away from its moorings. The sleek vessel slowly pulled away from the conglomerate of robots and EVA dock workers flying around tidying the spaceyard for the next ship.

"XO set course for clear space then to Rams Head System."

"Yes, Captain." The XO unbuckled his restraints and walked to the plot table to consult with the Navigator to set the course waypoints.

After three hours of shakedown to clear the gravity well, the *Versailles* jumped to the Rams Head System.

"Sensors?" Josephine asked.

"There is a ship on the system outskirts Captain, it's the *Grace* sir. No other contacts."

Josephine looked pointedly at her XO.

"Set an intercept course," she replied with a little trepidation.

"Aye, Aye."

♦ ♦ ♦

"Time to intercept the *Grace*, ten minutes."

Finding the Admiral in-system raised all sorts of questions. Captain La Perouse ordered another scan of the area before docking with the *Grace*. "Look for any hidden bases," she ordered. "XO, you're with me to welcome our guests. Harry, you have the conn," she said as she made her way off the bridge.

Several minutes later at the midship airlock, the Captain tapped her beeping comm. "Yes?"

The squeaky voice of her Sensor Operator came on, "Nothing, Captain. No contacts other than the *Grace*."

"Keep your eyes open," she said and cut the connection.

The hiss of air equalizing in the airlock ended as the *Versaille's* hatch clunked and whirled open. Captain La Perouse and her XO stood with uncertainty cast across their faces.

"Captain La Perouse," John said as the hatch swung far enough to reveal the Admiral and his entourage.

Why was the Admiral here in the middle of nowhere space? She had thought that she was being ostracized because it was common knowledge, amongst the growing numbers of ship's captains at Fleet HQ, her father had accused the Admiral of technology theft. Although nothing was ever proven, as far as she knew, either a sonic weapon was buried under red tape and the Secrecy Act, or her father was being obstinate. She didn't have any illusions that her father's name calling against the Admiral would be harmful to her career. She wasn't naive enough to believe her father's reputation didn't rub off on her. She didn't know the Admiral, but she did know her father.

"May I come aboard, Captain?"

"Bien sûr, mon Amiral," she replied in surprise as she slipped back into French.

"I assume that means okay Josephine," John said, his left eyebrow raised in mock consternation. "If I don't get these other two smell bags off the *Grace*, I may have a mutiny on my hands."

Josephine's face lit up with a slightly lopsided smile that accentuated her natural French beauty.

The stink from *Grace*'s airlock and crew wafted aboard with them. The air was foul, making the XO almost gag. Josephine inadvertently scrunched her nose just as Jen stepped forward through the hatch. Her somber face brooked no argument giving Josephine a pointed look before she asked where they could freshen up. Josephine's face drained of color, firstly with the Admiral's entry and now Commander Gale. Holding her breath, she nodded to the struggling XO to assign rooms for their smelly distinguished guests.

Suddenly the proximity alarm klaxon blared throughout the ship. That changed to a 'brace for impact' bell sound. The Captain and the XO, with eyes wide, turned back to the airlock.

"Shut that hatch!" she yelled to the Admiral, then turned and ran down the corridor as she tapped her earpiece comms. Jen and Max chuckled, looking at the quickly retreating backs of the funny little French Captain and XO as they bounced off the walls down the passageway. The floor grav-plating was currently set to low for routine minor maintenance.

When the Command Team filed onto the bridge, the Captain and XO turned abruptly toward them. Staring at the Admiral, Josephine ground her teeth, her face a mix of anger and curiosity.

He must have known all along that they were transporting a transit space station close by. Close enough to set off the proximity warning alarms putting the crew in a panic.

In the communique to Earth, John had requested that the station was placed in reasonable proximity, but not too close, to the Frigate. He had wanted to evaluate the crew's threat reaction to this new situation. It was out of self-interest; he wanted to be able to trust whoever came as their backup when they made alien contact.

John could see Max had disengaged the *Grace* as planned. The *Versailles's* shields and weapons were active. The two onboard Astro devils were flashing primed ready for launch. John walked the bridge checking the status of various systems nodding and shaking his head. Just as abruptly as when he entered, he addressed Josephine. "Very good Captain. I'd like an officers meeting at 1100 ST (Ship Time) after we've had time to freshen up and rest a little. In the meantime, please contact the station and render any assistance to station deployment." Titan shipyards had sent an inflatable space station. The station crew would need help to get it ready for use. John and his team left the bridge.

Josephine bit down on her comments. She could feel her face flush, she was furious on the inside. *I guess it's just what I should have expected from someone without honor.* She didn't quite go as far as thinking 'technology thief.'

Her XO surprised her when he commented, "Well, I guess we passed."

It took the Captain a minute to refocus and realize what the XO was saying. It was a readiness test. She made a mental note to herself that the Admiral was sneakier than she had originally anticipated. She also made a second note that the XO picked that up and she had not.

At 1100 the Captain's ready room was crowded with the Command Team and the *Versailles'* senior officers.

"Captain," John said with aplomb. "We, and I mean Humanity, are setting out on a new adventure. We have been ordered to gather intel and alien friends that are willing to ally with us, preferably without eating or enslaving us."

There was a murmur in the room.

"Rams Head station is to be a gateway station to other civilizations. It's far enough from Earth to make it difficult for aliens to detect where Earth is, adding an extra layer of security, but close enough to make trading with other species conveniently possible."

"I intend this station to become a clearinghouse for products to and from other species in the short term. At least until we establish our colonies in several dozen systems."

Once again, there was a murmur throughout the room.

"The *Versailles* will be one of many ships protecting Human space and assisting in the alien contact with other sentient species."

"Admiral, we are on our own out here, shouldn't we wait till those dozen colonies are set up before we come out here?" the XO said.

"No. I don't believe we have the time to wait. We need friends to help fight the Lizards when they return. Yes, it will be dangerous for the moment. We will be taking it cautiously, but we must start somewhere and soon. Our scientists can only reverse engineer so much in the short period we have before the next attack. We will need to buy weapons and the like to have any chance.

"Our mission is to contact sentient alien species to ally and hopefully start trade negotiations for technology," he continued as he made eye contact with the *Versailles* officers. "But first we need to set up the station with security, repair docks and trade center.

"Based on Squishy intel, we believe there is a trading hub out near Sirah System. This will be our first target once the scout recon finds it."

When John ended the meeting, he still hadn't told them that Humanity had to pick a fight with a powerful species first, to prove themselves.

Standing up and turning around the room, he remarked, "You all have a lot of work to do. Let's get to it."

♦♦♦

Two weeks later

By the time John and his team entered the command center of the space station, the station's implementation team and *Versailles* crew had deployed the solar panels and four external fuel tanks with heat pumps. Although they were still early in the deployment process, the station was capable. Both ships maneuvered near the docking corridor attached to the hangar and shuttled across. The T shaped corridor structure was attached to the main station with a gimbal snake to bridge the gap. The main station could rotate on several axes through the bridge leaving the hangar and docking corridor semi-fixed in space.

The four large solar collector wings jutted out the side of the platform facing the sun. Battery indicators showed all but two taking on power.

The solar collectors constituted part of the power system. The main power would come from two fusion reactors. The implementation team was hard at work, starting the first reactor.

"We have a green light for magnetic containment. Start pumping the lasers," said Professor Oleman, the foreman. The man had wily gray hair that sprung out like Einstein. Some had joked on his look-alike appearance; they only made that mistake once.

"Yes, Professor."

"Battery charge levels have passed the reactor ignition threshold. Fuel is loaded. Are we ready to light up the alpha reactor?"

A chorus of, "Yes, sir," came through the comm.

"Firing the peta lasers in five, four, three... fire." The Professor pressed the start button.

Within the reactor's magnetic containment chamber sixteen lasers fired in successive micro-pulses at the core of boron fuel, igniting it to fifty million degrees. Hundreds of pistons on the outside of the spherical chamber injected lithium hydride onto the magnetic containment field compressing it. The core temperature rose further to jump over one hundred and fifty million degrees.

The reactor relied on the compressors to inject electron stripped magnetized lithium hydride material into the boron plasma. In that instant, the fuel fused releasing large amounts of free-floating ions. The ovoid shape of the field pushed the ions out one end via an electrostatic funnel cathode that aligned the ion stream into an electrical current.

The Professor stood behind peering over the shoulder of a nervous technician. His temples dripped beads of sweat despite the comfortable temperature in the command module. Everyone held their breaths.

"Capacitors are charging," said the technician as he confirmed base power had switched on.

Cheers arose from the control room.

"Ready to switch from emergency battery power," said the Professor.

"Switching relays from batteries to the Alpha Reactor." The small power technician flicked open the clear plastic switch guard and pressed the red rocker button that changed color to green. The station power switched over to the fusion reactor as its source. Excess power from the grid would be diverted to the batteries if they were low on charge.

"Batteries are now taking on all current from the Alpha and solar panels F through J."

"Pump water in the ballast ring and rotate the station's gravity module." Small ion thrusters on the station gave a short burst to spin the station's outer reaches." The bulky older style station shifted, and the torus rotated slowly. Until the station was installed with gravity plating, one module would use centrifugal motion to create temporary gravity. It would become a sanctuary against weightlessness if the grav-projectors failed. The grav-projectors were power hogs and would normally only be switched on after the second reactor was powered up. The professor looked at the thruster response, satisfied that, if needed, the station could move out of the path of an incoming asteroid.

"Ok, light up the hangar," the Professor said.

A charged green glow materialized around the main hangar where the light curtain separated space from its interior deck.

"Ok, route power to the gravity projectors."

"Sir?" It was against normal protocol.

Professor Oleman looked over toward the Admiral's direction. The professor hated zero G. "Continue."

The docking ring and hangar sat stationary on a separate module with a space bridge between it and the rotating main bulk of the station. Jen pointed toward the dull gray opening as the lighting flickered on. It would allow the *Grace* to dock shortly after the initialization software had booted-up the environmentals. Several people in *Versailles* EVA suits flew around the station verifying the radiation shielding and sensors had been deployed correctly. As each module was inflated, a person would fly in and catalyze the skin with a flash from a lightning rod. By placing the rod against the pumped-up outer layer, the installer electrifies the special graphene A-Bitumen compound that insulates the station; the soft metal alloy would harden on contact with the electric current. The layers bonded to each other on a molecular level. Once the outer structural layer was assembled, an internal module is slid inside before it's fastened to the rest of the station. Slowly the hours crept by as the station took shape.

Further modules would be delivered to build a liquid oxygen storage facility and a basic ship repair yard that housed mechanical spider bots.

"Have the shields and the defense suite been deployed?"

John turned at the silence, his stare could cut diamond.

"Umm not yet Admiral, we wanted to make sure you were comfortable first," said the Professor who gulped with mild apprehension.

John's eyes narrowed, zeroing in on the man. "You *will* follow standard deployment protocols. Those protocols were tested and are there for a reason. If you can't follow them, I'll get someone who will."

The Professor swallowed.

John pressed his com for the *Versailles*. "Captain, this is Admiral Stevenson, please set and stay at amber alert until the station's weapons and defense shielding has been deployed."

"Yes, Admiral."

John stared once more at the Professor then turned and left the command center without looking back.

Jen smiled at the Professor and scurried after John.

"You can be a bit abrasive sometimes," she said as she caught up.

John's head snapped around. "It was foolish of him to set our comfort above station security."

"There are no ships other than ours in the system," Jen said frowning.

"But they're out there!" he said waving his arm in all directions before storming off.

The station still had a lot of modules to install before it was functional enough to say it was a working station.

Jen stood in the corridor with her arms around her body, watching as John disappeared towards the hanger bay. Was it just John's paranoia? Was he cracking?

Chapter 17

Max's Station, Titan Orbit

Mags leaned up against the large windows of the observation lounge, studying the turbulent weather patterns on Saturn's largest moon, Titan. Memories of her Basic Dirt training flooded back, making her smile.

She was excited at the challenges of the new assignment on Rams Head Station; she had never thought she would actually go to another star system. Exciting wasn't the first thought Mags had at the prospect of traveling through parsecs of dark space. Everyone knew the vacuum of space was a dangerous place. Mags wasn't fond of the dark either, not even close.

Out the window everything needed to be lit with floodlights to warn pilots and suited workers doing EVA's around the station. Colored lights sat motionless relative to the station markers which delineated the space lanes and flight no-go zone boundaries.

Max's Station was primarily a T.N. military base that was morphing into a commercial hub with Intersolar and interstellar craft transiting through it.

Mags had read the history of its construction; it was the first T.N. space station built when the lizard abductions started. It seemed incredible to her that the five founding members of T.N. had achieved so much, including setting up the bare bones to the behemoth she now sat in. The station superstructure was immense.

Mags turned to face the edge of the clear portal. Out of the black, she saw lights flicker on down the spine of an enormous ship coming into view. It was the interstellar freighter *T.M.N. Aneska,* her ride to Rams Head Station.

Mags watched the massive ship burn its maneuvering thrusters to synchronize the hull speed with the station's docking corridor. Two sky bridges telescoped out from the corridor taking up two separate platform entrances. The bow entrance of the vessel held the command bridge and crew quarters, then there was a spindly cylindrical spine corridor with containers attached radiating out all around. The stern module housed the main reactor and the two electro plasma Mark II engines. Much of the spine of the ship was configured for cargo containers this voyage. She had read that aside from a small corridor giving crew access to the engine module far to the rear, the containers joined together and formed its backbone, giving it structural rigidity.

Fluoro-suited cargo handlers whisked about on small sleds cajoling containers destined for Max's Terminal. The bulk of the cargo had been loaded on Earth then sent through Hope and now Max's Station before going interstellar to Rams Head Station. Her natural curiosity led her to try to find the star they were traveling to, but the astrogation data was a tightly kept secret. So, Mags picked a star in the constellation of the Ram to focus on.

Twenty minutes later there was a murmur around the lounge; a young man in a black merchant navy uniform with shoulder patches for the *Aneska* was jostled at the bar for gossip.

A chime sounded alerting people to the ship status boards in the center of the lounge ceiling. The status for the *Aneska* at gate 23 and gate 24 changed to green and showed the freighter was ready for boarding and preparing to depart.

Mags felt her pulse quicken as the pad in her pocket vibrated. She pulled it out to see she had orders to report to the freighter *Aneska* at dock 23. Mags straightened her tunic and picked up her duffel to make her way through the crowd. She heard excited snippets of conversations saying this was the *Aneska's* first trip to Rams Head and how dangerous it was. She thought the space enthusiasts would have been all over the new destination. Despite this and the station staff knowing the existence of the new station, Mags hadn't seen anything in the social media.

Mags walked down the docking corridor while she counted the docks, verifying it with the airlock gate numbers. Up ahead, she saw the self-same man from the bar waving her forward.

"You must be Lt. Hanks?"

"Yes, sir," Mags said as she glanced at his collar. The man wore a single silver bar but had two black lines etched in it: he outranked her.

"I'm Lt. Banks but call me Artie. Come aboard, I'll show you to C deck. You'll have to bunk with the crew because we don't have a passenger module this run."

"Yes, sir."

"Normally as an officer, you'd get a cabin," he smiled as he shrugged, "but we have a Comm specialist traveling as-well who claimed it first."

"It's no problem. How long is the trip?"

"It'll take a few days to get out of the gravity well, then we'll drop into subspace for a bit. We should be there in three and a half days."

"Oh, I thought it would be a lot quicker with the sub-space thingy."

Artie laughed, "Subspace thingy..." then shook his head. "Like warp drive, I suppose."

Mags nodded.

Artie shook his head once again. Taking a closer look at Mag's creamy skin.

Mags caught him perving at her skin, and raised an eyebrow.

"You're not a spacer?" he said embarrassed.

Mags frowned at the comment, *what does that mean?*

"No offense, your skin is very pale but not spacer pale."

Mags stared. "Yes, and no. I've been in space nearly a year now." Mags pursed her lips. *I know he's going to lord it over me for sure.*

Artie, spotting her expression, held up his hands defensively.

"So how long on have you been on ..." Mags waved around at the walls of the freighter.

"Just over a year," he said smugly. "But she's been in service longer than that."

"How fast does the ship go, warp 3, 4?"

Artie stopped and scrutinized her, evaluating what he could tell, then smiled. "The 'Neska is a slow old girl. She has the legs to get there but only uses them when she's in a real hurry."

Artie showed Mags to the crew quarters where she dumped her duffle on the bed and stowed her valuables in her locker. "Mess ends at 1300 today because we're pulling out at 1800. In there is the refresher," he pointed. "Follow me, and I'll introduce you to the Captain. He can answer your questions."

Mags looked at him curiously.

Artie continued. "Everybody new has questions on shipboard ops. Some things aboard are classified, like the drives or spider bots because they are working to commercialize and license them. So, we're told."

Mags nodded; it made sense.

The two passed the galley entrance as delicious aromas wafted from inside. "You'll like the food; the Captain spared no expense getting the chef."

The two passed through several hatches before entering a corridor where Artie knocked on a small wooden looking door.

"Enter." A pleasant but muffled voice answered.

Artie lead Mags into the Captain's ready room to stand before his desk. Off to the side, in an adjoining room, she could see a single bunk and a picture of the Grand Canyon above it.

"Captain, this is Lt. Hanks."

An older man with grey streaks in his hair looked up and scrutinized Mags. She could tell the man was used to command as he smiled.

"Take a seat, Lieutenant. Drink?"

Turning to her guide, the Captain said, "Artie, would you get a few cokes?" The Captain shifted his attention back to Mags with a raised eyebrow.

Mags nodded. "Thank you, Captain."

"Is this your first-time aboard ship?"

"An interstellar one, yes, sir."

"Artie will get you some reading materials and go through the safety protocols."

"Yes, sir."

"Do you know much about Rams Head?" he asked.

"No, sir, not a lot, just that it's new. I'm going as security."

That surprised Artie and the Captain until they had a closer look at Mags's certs on her uniform. Both had assumed she was science, and she was going there for the lab construction.

Ten minutes later, Mags and Artie had left the Captain's cabin for a tour of the ship and the basics of finding the nearest lifepod.

♦♦♦

Crew Berthing, *T.M.N. Aneska*

Despite the novelty of new surroundings, after the tour Mags spent a lot of her time on her bunk studying space station security protocols. Each night the crew would gather in the mess to relax and socialize. Twice during the leg out of the gravity well, they had a practice emergency. Mags was familiar with space suits and skin suits they used in the drills, but when Artie spent extra time assisting her drill, she smiled. Aside from that, her time was her own. She thought it might not be so bad working for a living in the merchant navy. By the third day, she had adjusted to the shipboard routine. There were watch standers 24 /7 on the bridge. Artie got the dog watch, so Mags would sometimes visit the bridge in the early hours to keep him and the Helm company. The *Aneska* had a crew of twenty but could be flown with as few as three in a pinch.

"Lt. Hanks to the bridge."

Mags stopped mid-sentence on a report; she quickly stowed her laptop and raced toward the bow.

"I thought you might like to see this. Strap yourself in tactical while we dock," the Captain said as he pointed to the main viewer. Rams Head station was coming into view.

Mags could see the bones of the new station. There was a lot still in the dark. Off to one side was a docking corridor like the one she had seen on Max's Station. The far end of the corridor snaked its way into the darkness. Much of the station still looked unfinished with construction arms outstretched. Sleds that were lit up like Christmas trees flitted back and forth preparing for the *Aneska* to dock.

"Thank you, Captain. I guess that hunk of metal is home sweet home for a while."

Artie chuckled in the background.

Mags watched the whole docking procedure from the back of the *Aneska's* bridge. When the Captain spoke up, "Mags, you're free to disembark."

Mags took a breath before she floated around the bridge to shake the crew's hands thanking them for the ride and for them to have a safe journey on to Cresseda.

The whole trip had seemed surreal until now; the gourmet meals, pleasant company and the well-equipped gym made the voyage more like a resort cruise liner than a cargo transport.

♦♦♦

Mags stepped through the airlock into station air which had a cold, bitter metallic taste.

She smiled as she approached a short man with fizzy Einstein hair that stood near the airlock. "Lt. Hanks? You the only passenger?"

Mags shook her head. "There's a systems specialist, a Mr. Rajin."

The wirily man waved off her response.

"Damn, they were supposed to pick up an accommodation module with another twenty staff. What am I supposed to do with a security beef and a comm efficiency expert? You are both less than useless to me right now," he said, not registering how insulting he sounded.

Mags stared at him. That was not what the Security Director had told her. It was too late now, so she didn't say anything.

Mags was getting ticked off at this person. "Who are you?"

"I'm Professor Oleman, Station Administrator, your Boss," he said proudly. "There's only a few of us, so you better pull your weight on the menial stuff."

Mags thought about getting back on the *Aneska*.

The man walked quickly down the corridor without waiting on a response. Mags shook her head and raced to catch up as he took her through turn after turn of the station. It was clear from the inside there was a lot of work to do. Even though the corridor was lit, many of the panels or door access points were without power.

"Stow your gear there," he said, pointing to a cabin door at the end of the corridor. "Don't touch anything not turned on. In fact, don't touch anything period. The security module is not yet operational, so find me after you have settled in. I must rush, the *Aneska* is dumping her cargo and running. I need to go to the control room to make sure the cargo slobs put it where we want it, and not tumbling off toward the belt." He turned and trotted quickly back the way they had come.

Mags walked to her cabin and sat on the bed alcove, the room was small but serviceable. Director Withers had said it was only a short assignment; she hoped he was right. Mags unpacked her duffel, anchored her laptop to the desk then set out through unfamiliar corridors to find the Station Administrator.

Chapter 18

Grace's Bridge, Outskirts Rams Head System

John sent scouts out to systems beyond Rams Head; mostly in the direction of Sirah System and the trader stations. There were thousands of stars between Sirah and RHS. So far there had been no sign of E.T. at any planet or system visited by scouts or probes. Frustrated, he took the *Grace* to explore some of the systems toward Sirah himself.

John checked the status of the power draw made by the gravity projectors to form and stabilize the bubbles surrounding the *Grace*. He knew Jen was monitoring them, but he couldn't help himself checking. She was trialing different configurations of gravity models since the success of her outrigger setup in the Tau Ceti System.

Some of her grav configurations had been downright nasty. They had nearly torn the ship apart. John really didn't want to be a crash test dummy, but he trusted Jen not to kill them.

Today they had a variant of the tri outrigger model where three torpedo-shaped grav bubbles attached near the ship's structural supports that held them together. It stabilized the *Grace* as it tore through space warped by the bow gravity projectors and the gas giant in the system. The torpedo bubbles were dynamic, shifting density with the changes in the gravity fields.

Their recent stop-over at Rams Head Station (RHS) provided their energy collectors time to top up the batteries.

Tela had pointed John and Jen toward the Sirah system almost 300 light years from Rams Head. They should encounter other species at the space trading station there or close by. Setting up Rams Head as a forward base was merely the first step towards contact with other advanced species. Any trouble and they could return there without endangering Earth.

The station would be either purged of any information that was not heavily encrypted and could be used to locate Earth. There was no doubt that their continued anonymity was one of their greatest defenses.

They set *Grace's* acceleration briefly at four gravities on their flight out of the system. Rams Head station was positioned on the edge of the sun's and gas giant's gravity well. This meant ships that used the Alcubierre drive (A-

Drive) could do a fast turnaround; they could transition from subspace to normal space, complete their trade and be off back into subspace without having to enter or exit a deep gravity well. The *Grace* disappeared from RHS to materialize at the first waypoint system toward Sirah System.

"Engaging A-drive." The *Grace* pushed its fusion reactors and transitioned into subspace. Within the cargo hold sat a dozen special stealth probes to be placed in systems along the route. Their grav and plasma-interferometers would measure wave disturbances created by an Alcubierre drive. They could tell if an FTL ship passed near the system.

The special probes also had a small jump drive inside to link to the next probe in a daisy chain from RHS to the alien trade center. The probe's drive would, on command, transport non-jump capable ships or comm buoys to and from the trade center through the chain of probes. It could also act as an automatic relay point for any emergency jumps, sending the ship on to the next waypoint toward RHS then Sol if necessary.

"Three, two, one ... Mark!" The *Grace* materialized a light week's distance from the waypoint star system, HD22765. This was their first of five waypoints to Sirah where they would deploy one of the special jump capable stealth probes.

Clear Space Waypoint 3 to Sirah System

"Are we clear to drop out of FTL?" John asked. Despite having done it hundreds of times, John stuck to the routine of using the A-drive coming to and leaving any system. He believed he couldn't be too careful to give the illusion of Humanity only having Alcubiere-drive (A-Drive) technology.

"Yes!" the two chorused.

John transitioned the *Grace* from its subspace bubble to normal space.

Small chimes echoed throughout the bridge, drawing attention to three ship contacts as the tachyon scanners cleared.

"Max, what have we got?"

"Three contacts 06 degrees, 320 decl. (declination), at three light minutes."

"Damn, they're close. Ok, light 'em up with active scans."

Max swiveled the active tachyon scanner towards the contacts.

"They're on an intercept course, three light minutes and closing. They're frigate class; the design is different from that of the Squishy traders, they have different reactor and pulse emissions."

"How soon before they are in laser range?"

"Based on our heavy mk3 lasers, they'll be in range in 15 minutes. But it's hard to know what armaments they have at this distance. We've got twelve more large ships on the scope."

John and Jen held their breaths. John wondered why they weren't in subspace.

"I think they're freighters. The frigates must be their escort."

"Any Comms from them?"

"No."

"Steering away from the convoy," John said as he adjusted the helm control. *Maybe showing them, we're not a threat... Damn!* John thought they didn't have enough time to recharge the jump drive. He sounded general quarters then, with grav assist, turned the ship 90° and ordered engineering to reinitialize the A-drive.

They would need to drop back into subspace. It was their best alternative at the moment.

The reactor in *Grace*'s mid-ship gave a noticeable tremor as they skipped it to quicken the energy build up. It normally took time to generate the minimum power requirement for a shift into FTL. By skipping the reactor, they would boost it to a higher output immediately but damage it in the process.

"Captain, did you say skip?" came a voice back from engineering.

"Yes, we have warships, inbound."

"Aye, sir."

John turned his face to the main holo-view. "Enemy in range in ten minutes." He knew this was based on current lizard technology.

John saw the drive energy recharge indicator creep slowly from amber towards the green.

"Max, let me know if you get any energy readings that the enemy is charging their weapons or locking on us."

John pressed the comm to engineering, "Lieutenant, can you get any more out of that reactor, the enemy will be in range in five minutes."

"Admiral, I don't know what else to say, but it's redlining; it's running at 120% max. I'll only be able to maintain that for one-hour 'n twenty minutes."

"Max, bring up the lidar scans, let's see what we can figure out." The scans were blurry images of the convoy a half hour before the *Grace* had arrived in system. The three frigates flew in an equilateral triangle formation. They were well coordinated.

"Jen, where is the emergency jump drive targeted to?" The *Grace* had two jump drives. One was always kept charged as an emergency drive.

"I've set it to daisy chain through to Rams Head Station." They couldn't jump to Earth directly because it was too far.

John switched 50% of the power being generated from the reactor to the shields.

"Jen, set up the new skin shield."

The *Grace* had been upgraded with a new fusion reactor and a heavier shield projector before she left Earth. The extra projectors were dual-layered and would enable it to fine-tune the shields. The new enhanced computer algorithms were to create high-speed shield frequency rotation and power management. The shield projectors also created a second inner harmonic shield in an undulating waveform that hugged the hull forming a second skin that shimmered with multispectral colors. Like a pianist playing a chord, the second shield was a harmonic of the primary. Tests confirmed that the practice would give almost 20% more protection given the same power. A secondary benefit, the second shield was masked under the first creating an overall smaller energy footprint. It was all due to new fields theory with quantum computer control. Humanity's computer technology was rapidly leveling the technology gap. As long as the aliens didn't get their hands on the computer tech. Minicomputer controlled mobile projectors scooted over the hull, creating or reinforcing where necessary.

As the shields came online, John could see only a minor drop in their speed.

Gnoll Lord Volund's Frigate, *Light Bringer*

Lord Volund sat on his command chair squinting at the grainy monochromatic image of his sister. "Is it worth our time on the small ship?" asked Lord Volund over the comm to his sister who flew directly in front of him in her own ship, the *Wild Roar*. His sister, Lord Saga, was a pacer like many felines. She paced back and forth on the bridge to relieve her nerves while they were in pursuit of their prey. It made talking to her mid-battle frustrating. Volund tapped his cat claws on the well-worn side rest, highlighting his irritation.

"I need a new yacht, besides once we do it up it'll be a glorious fashion statement. Cousin Vitapurr will be sooo jealous," Saga chuckled with a capricious grin, as she grinned her canines breached her lips.

"I like it when the little ships try to run, it makes the hunt more satisfying," boasted Lord Egress, the third lord captain of the last warship escorting the convoy.

"Lord Egress, you should stay with the freighters, in case this is a trap."

The Gnoll Lord held Volund's gaze, "No, I will not be excluded from the hunt. You stay if you are so concerned. You're the youngest of us all."

Volund gritted his molars. He was the youngest in age but the one with the greatest tactical experience. "At least hold off until we can target their engines. Look how weak their shields are. It is no competition against one of our ships, let alone three."

The three Gnoll warships trailing the *Grace* closed in quickly. "Glom, deep scan the yacht," Lord Volund ordered in a deep baritone. The scarred one-eyed Ferret sitting at tactical shifted and targeted the yacht.

Light Bringer's sensors spewed EM pulses that ran a detailed scan on the *Grace* to identify the ship and its technology. However, it was brought up short as it struck the inner shield.

"Lord, we cannot penetrate the hull," said the scared Ferret. The Ferret had lost his left eye when he was on the receiving end of an angry Gnoll's claw.

"Why, what's it made of?" growled Volund.

Glom licked his lips. "The spectral analysis does not return any reading."

Volund stared at the Ferret, his curiosity piqued. "Continue."

"Umm, there is a second shield beneath the first."

That caught Volund by surprise. Controlling shield projectors was a difficult task. Only those with fine motor skills could do it. The value of the aliens just jumped up in Volund's economic view. "Open a com to *Wild Roar* only."

"You won't believe this, but that ship has two shields, the second is so close to the hull it's as if it's part of the structure." Lord Volund passed that information to his older sibling.

Saga stopped midstride to look at the tactical screen. "How sneaky of the little ship." Lord Saga licked her lips.

Suddenly Volund's eyes widened, "Whoa, look at that ship turn..."

Bridge, *T.N. Grace*

"Evasive maneuvers, alpha 10 port," John said, as much a warning to the crew as the computer took the command to execute.

The little ship flipped over as he made a sharp turn without disrupting their acceleration.

John smiled as the three larger warships attempted to turn as sharply as the *Grace* to nearly collide in the process. John hadn't even used any gravity assist. Well, not much anyway. The projectors auto dampened the effects of inertia around the ship, so they weren't spread like jam on the bulkheads when they turned.

Alarms blared as the *Graces'* shields were struck with a poorly aimed laser shot. The graze was enough to make their rear shield light up like a green neon sign in a dark alley.

"Two LiDAR sensors are offline," said a disembodied computer voice.

The *Grace* began to pull away at right angles to the three cumbersome Frigates as they attempted to follow the small ship slaloming back and forth.

Small, fast low yield missiles flew out from two of the warships to strike against *Grace's* shields in a blaze of sparks and electrical fire.

"Point defense is not working! Engineering?"

There was no response except, "Working on it."

John cut their forward thrust, pulsed the maneuvering thrusters that flipped *Grace* to target the closest ship. In the space of a few seconds, he fired the main forward turret and flipped the ship back to its original course. The forward laser was their largest ship-based weapon they had, given the reactor size on the *Grace*.

Shields on the closest ship blazed with iridescent blue.

Lord Egress's shields lit up from the small ship's laser fire. Smaller explosions on *Tallos the Blade* signaled the destruction of several shield projectors on Egress's ship.

The Volund smiled at the grainy green picture displaying the other two ship Captains as the hunt became more interesting with every evasive maneuver.

"It appears the little ship has a nip. That weapon took 15% of your forward shields in one hit, Egress." Volund chuckled.

"It was a lucky shot," the older feline Lord growled, his fur disheveled from the laser's aftershock.

The *Grace's* shields flared again as the trailing ships fired their main laser cannons. The remaining 80% of her shields were blown away in one direct hit leaving the hull scored. The excess electromagnetic energy struck two recycler armor plates that housed two inches of a new compound. The energy was filtered and sluiced to a refractive heat sink that scattered then converted the excess EM energy into electrical energy and through redirect conduits sent it into the battery capacitors filling them. The armor was a one-use recharge, rendering it useless against another shot.

The ship shook violently, tossing the crew painfully against their harnesses. Somehow within the bridge compartment, they could smell the reek of burnt plastic and molten metal bitumen.

John could hear Jen scream with the violent shaking in the bridge. He slammed his hand on the A-drive engage button. The ship wobbled while the forward projectors whined as the ship slipped into subspace.

Bridge, Gnoll Frigate, *Light Bringer*

"Ha, the ship lost most of its shields," the Volund let out a deep snorting laugh. "It is dropping into subspace... Follow it!" The three wicked looking warships powered up their FTL drives and slipped into subspace, clamoring in pursuit. Flying in subspace was like steering a supertanker. Although the ship traveled enormous distances, turning was a bitch, it was possible but difficult to achieve without enormous amounts of energy to redirect the inertia. John steered the ship towards a nearby star.

"Max, are they still following us?"

"Yes, this new sensor that Pete came up with is amazing." Max instantly regretted it, seeing the pained look that flashed across John's face.

"Do you think they can shoot at us in subspace?" Jen asked, worriedly. Her front teeth bit lightly into her bottom lip.

"I don't know if their senses are as good as ours. My gut feeling is they are, they can probably see us well enough to track us and maybe even target us."

"Shouldn't we use the jump drive now, that last shot nearly wiped us out!" Jen said, emphatically.

"Jen," John said, "I'm worried, but I want to drop around behind something big before we make the jump. Max, is there any way to contact the *Versailles*?"

"No, we're on our own."

John inadvertently winced before he realized that both Jen and the Chief Engineer's holo-image were looking directly at him. He couldn't worry about that now, he steeled himself to focus. Sitting still, he formulated a plan.

"Well done Chief, that little extra power got us up over the line and started the A-drive... "

John was beaming from ear to ear when the Chief lost his own enormous smile as he was abruptly knocked to the floor. "Oh damn, they're still behind us."

"Jen, I need the gravity projectors online, once we bolt around the sun. I need you to activate it as strong as you can sunward side. We'll use the extra mass for a grav assist in slingshotting us." Calculating the engine impulse to change their direction for the deep space maneuver was going to be a nightmare.

Jen had created gravity bubbles to help them turn the ship before, but not when they were so close to the system's sun. She flipped her second screen to show an app she created to guide her bubble's force vectors versus the background gravity on their sensors. Jen shook her head, this was crazy. She wasn't sure the *Grace* would hold together or that the gravity bubbles would maintain their surface tension integrity.

The three ships trailed the *Grace*, steadily gaining on her. It would not be long before one of their shots rattled more than just the dust off the shelves.

John steered the ship directly down the gullet of the star's gravity well hoping the enemy frigates would disengage.

◆◆◆

Bridge, Gnoll Frigate, *Wild Roar*

"This little ship is slipperier than your belly when you crawl on your knees to me, Volund!" chided the large muscle-bound female Gnoll. The adrenalin of the chase was kicking in.

"It's slipping into subspace, follow it!" she snarled to the helm.

"Yes, mistress." There was a tremble in the little Ferret's voice. His whiskers twitched echoing his fear.

The Gnoll laughed aloud. She would get this vessel. Her whole demeanor bordered on the maniacal. Her gladiatorial standing within Gnoll gentry was barely enough to make the lordly rankings where social status relied on warranted feats of strength, intelligence, economic cunning, or outright mighty power.

The Gnoll were a Servant predatory species that only recognized other species of the same caliber. Their thought pattern forced them to either outright dominate other advanced civilizations for their social ranking pleasure, or run far and fast. Many wondered about their insectoid Patron, the Sil'thik. Nobody knew how the Gnoll was subjugated by them given their fight or flight nature.

Lord Saga had had a tough several years, especially after losing the right to attend the King's Chamber of Lords to her childhood nemesis and younger brother, Lord Volund. Although born from the same parents, she denied his male superiority as becoming an adult Gnoll dictated. Her brother's cavernous mouth had yelled long and loud of his accomplishments, which overshadowed Saga's own despite her greater number of years.

"Well, little sister, are you sure that this bug ship is small enough for you! Such a tiny ship may get lost underfoot by accident. I would hate to have to get a microscope to find your body," Volund jeered.

"Volund, that will be difficult when I am on top of your foot." Saga countered over the transmission.

The two siblings bantered with exaggerated one-up-man-ship, as the three ships relentlessly pursued the little Human vessel through subspace.

"Do not shoot to destroy, let me take this vessel with minimal damage!" Saga ordered the two competing Captains.

"I won't let you take all the riches of this strange species," yelled Egress. When Volund and Saga had volunteered to escort the freighter convoy, Egress had tagged along with them to build his own social standing.

His contemptuous drawl was open for all to see as he tried to take the yacht for himself.

Egress's claims ran partially true; if Saga captured the small ship, and from it the location of a new species to subjugate, she would win handsomely. It would fast-track Saga to the chamber of lords, where she would also get an enormous commission from the sale of the slaves, technology, and commerce that would accrue from such an introduction to their prey's homeworlds. Egress wanted that commission.

Volund knew that his sister was overbearing in this case. He also knew that she needed a boost to her social standing much more than he did. He was willing to forego his share but could not see Lord Egress being so generous. So Volund decided to interfere with the interloper's targeting in his pursuit of this little alien ship.

Before Volund was able to maneuver his ship to thwart the egocentric Lord Egress, the tiny alien ship made an unbelievably tight turn within subspace. This was unheard of as inertia pulled the ships at impossible speeds. It was like turning a supertanker on a dial at speed. The little ship's value just jumped into the stratosphere: technology like that would change the way the Gnoll race fought ship to ship battles.

"Drop and spin, quickly!" Volund yelled. They had to drop from subspace, turn the frigate then return to subspace on the new heading. The maneuver was not uncommon, but it took time. "My lord, we cannot, we are deep within the gravity well."

Volund growled. The ferret was right.

The three trailing ships doggedly followed the lead of the Human ship. Their superior engines allowed them to gain distance lost by the alien ship's unbelievable evasive maneuvers.

"What's it doing?! It's heading directly for that star! We must capture it before it's destroyed in the gravity well," shouted Saga.

While she was yelling the other two ships had already scolded their engineering crew to give them more speed, pushing their two ships in front of Saga's. Volund's ship caught up so quickly that it almost grappled the little ship.

"Give me more power to the drives you idiots!" Saga yelled at her own engineering crew. The crew jumped to her bidding.

♦♦♦

Bridge, *T.N. Grace*

"Now, Jen!" John said.

Jen looked back with trepidation then activated the strong gravity bubble surrounding the ship, neutralizing the worst of the inertia effects. John risked everything and dropped out of subspace extremely close to the star. Normally any ship dropping from subspace near a star would be ripped apart. The star's gravity grabbed the small ship in its bubble and tossed it like flotsam in the surf. Jen powered the mobile shield projectors to strengthen the small multispectral bubble surrounding the ship, giving it more strength. The added strength inadvertently stretched the bubble's boundaries. Despite the sun's sheer mass, the bubble protected them from the huge gravimetric forces of the gravity well.

"A little more ..." The *Grace* skirted the sun's purple corona as flares spewed from its surface. Radiation blasted the *Grace* and interfered with her sensors making the Gnoll ships vanish off their scope. John slammed his hand on the jump drive dematerializing the *Grace*. The small ship groaned as the grav bubble warped space ripping it through the jump drive.

♦♦♦

Bridge, Gnoll Frigate, *Wild Roar*

Lord Saga's crew's slow reaction saved their lives as the little ship that flew directly into the gravity well, suddenly disappeared.

♦♦♦

Bridge, Gnoll Frigate, *Light Bringer*

In that instant aboard the *Light Bringer*, Volund experienced the biggest mystery of his life... How did the little ship counteract the extreme forces of gravity generated by the sun and the FTL drive when it dropped from subspace? He did not know what the answer was before his ship flew into the aftermath of the gravity wave equalization.

An enormous burst of energy ripped space-time jumping the little ship from near the star. The bubble of zero gravity that surrounded the *Grace* created a turbulent backflow at its boundary. The *Grace*'s wake dragged the two closer ships from the gravity convergence boundary spitting them out near their prey in Rams Head System.

Chapter 19

T.N. Grace, near Rams Head Station

The *Grace* emergency jump passed through the daisy chain of probes and rematerialized in Rams Head system near the *Versailles* and the new RHS space station. They had teleported through two waypoints one hundred and twenty-five lightyears from the unnamed (designated HP99012) Star System where the battle took place. Space buckled as the gravity differential from teleporting near a star forced it to explosively surge out in an expanding sphere that rippled through Rams Head space to shove the *Versailles* and the Rams Head station away from the focus of rematerialization zone.

The sudden appearance of the *Grace* sent shockwaves that rippled the fabric of space/time, straight through the *Versailles'* hull. Without shields, the ship buckled, the electromagnetic bracing within the bulkheads sheared, fracturing the keel in half. Corridors and partitions ruptured as breaches in the bitumen hardened hull spewed vital air into space. The crew were tossed like rag dolls.

The space station would have suffered a similar fate, had it not been conducting shield tests just as the *Grace* dropped back to normal space. Large areas of the station's hard surface were bashed in, dented and damaged, despite the protective shielding. The sanctuary module was ripped from its housing, spewing vital air into space.

Jen cut the power to the gravity bubble just as *Grace's* ship-net connected to the RHS Wi-fi and downloaded auto sensor reports. Screen after screen poured in from the station and frigate. Blocks of red warning status filled her screen. Jen was stunned at the devastation that befell her.

"Holy crap, John!"

Bridge, *T.N. Versailles*

Battered and bruised Josephine rolled over to see her XO crawling towards the jump controls. She gritted her teeth as pain seared her chest and lower left leg. She was sure she had cracked or broken ribs, not to mention a splitting headache. She could hear distant clanging. It was important, but her mind was too foggy to do anything but register it. Then through the pain as if in a dream, she watched the determined young XO reach the emergency jump control guard and slam his fingers down onto the red EJP execute button. The jump drive whined as darkness descended around the Captain when she slipped unconscious.

Chapter 20

Emergency Jump Platform, Titan

Alarms blared soon after the *Versailles* materialized on the Emergency Jump Platform (EJP). The EJP was an aired-up, zero-G chamber set up to receive ships in distress. Emergency and Security services came floating in to find the *Versailles's* dented and damaged hull. Vice Admiral Dunn was notified with a priority-one message that a ship had materialized within the EJP.

"Which ship is it?" He demanded of the Captain who was attempting to pick up any transponder that was active in the wreck of a ship.

"Sir, it's the *Versailles*, I'm trying to download its last departure point, but the computers must be damaged!"

The Versaille was supposed to be John's backup! Dammit, what happened? Jason nodded once, trying not to harass the Captain for more information. He was obviously busy attempting to get what he could, pestering him wouldn't help, so he sat back in his chair. Breathing deeply so as not to get too worked up, it was difficult for Jason to push down his worry. He knew that they had no jump capable warships available to assist John; he amended his thoughts to include the *Grace* and all her crew.

The only ships jump capable were the battle carrier with its escort, which would have to remain within the Sol System for Earth's defense and those on patrol out in the colonies. They could send a jump merchant vessel, or jump control can send a non-jump capable ship that would be stranded there. Jason checked the status of available merchant navy ships. The *T.M.N. Aneska* was a jump capable freighter and had just returned to Sol system from Traynor.

Jason commed the T.N. Merchant Dept Head. "Abigail, we have an emergency. I'll need to commandeer the *Aneska*."

Abigail nodded at Jason's request. "They are uploading Agricultural machinery at Dragon Trees cargo terminal." Dragon Trees was a spaceport hub in Western Australia.

Jason shifted gears and turned to his subordinate, "Captain, have a SAR team report to the *Aneska* at Dragon Trees cargo terminal."

"Yes, sir," he said distractedly.

The *T.N. Invictus* was undergoing the security upgrade; *T.N. Minerva and T.N. Pax* were on patrol around the colonies. Jason was annoyed at John for stretching their resources to the limit with his 'trade mission.' He would have words with him about commandeering their limited stock of warships. He knew that these negative thoughts were just because he had an uncomfortable lack of options.

"Find out if the *Grace* is docked inside the *Versailles'* hangar bay!"

Ten minutes later the Captain responded, "There were no ships in the hangar bay, only their runabout shuttle."

Thank God the Grace wasn't inside her, what the hell happened?

Half an hour later, Jason asked his aide, "Are the SARs on their way to the *Aneska*?"

"Yes, sir."

Jason then had another thought. Maybe the *Scotty* can help.

"Where's the *Scotty* now?" The Captain's fingers whizzed over his console, searching for the latest flight plan for the famous Angel ship. The Captain was surprised when he saw the destination, "The last known flight plan made by the *Scotty* was towards the Canopus system."

"It's one of the brightest stars in the southern hemisphere." The Captain leaned into his monitor to try and clear his mind and focus on the *Versailles*. His face showed he was clearly disturbed.

"What else can you tell me about that star system, Captain." Jason could see the Captain cringe.

"Well, some believe that Canopus is linked to the concept of life and death. Ancient mariner's lore has it being used as a navigational marker to the *underworld*.

The Captain looked at Jason, then returned to his screen, setting priorities for the SAR team assigned to the *Versailles*.

Jason took that on board with trepidation as he silently wished Elvis and his team luck in navigating the stars.

Bridge, *T.N. Grace*, Rams Head System

Jen looked at John in horror as the battered *Versailles* dematerialized. She hoped they jumped successfully back to the Emergency Jump Platform (EJP) in Sol System. Jen hated to think what it would have been like on the inside the ship. How many had she killed by jumping too close to the frigate and the space station? They had never jumped in the middle of grav assist maneuver, especially when the energy of the grav assist was extreme as it was so close to the star. Stunned at the implication of the release of pent-up energy, the combined effect was devastating.

The last time she had felt this horrible sinking feeling, this utter dread, was when their dog Scotty had been killed by ole man Sykes. Jen had accidentally teleported half of the man to space without a suit.

John was equally shocked at the devastation that played out before him. Luckily the *Versailles* jumped out: if they couldn't, they would have been in far more trouble he rationalized.

They could do nothing for the *Versailles* right now, so he had to focus on the station.

"Damn!" John cursed. Grav projectors and the sensors were offline. He had forgotten to retract them when he jumped.

"Max, open a comm, I want to talk to the station commander."

"Rams Head space station this is the *T.N. Grace,* please respond?"

"John, there's no response on any band," Max said.

"There's still shielding over the hangar bay, we're not going to be able to land. Jen, see if we can target one of the areas that's unshielded for a teleport." Jen didn't respond, she was caught up in her own thoughts. "Jen! Snap out of it! We need to get to that station ASAP. Are you with me?" John barked loudly at Jen.

Snapping her head around towards John, her eyes narrowed without saying a word. Max could hear her teeth grind, and winced, glad he wasn't in John's shoes right now.

"Fine..." Jen retorted.

"Max, I need you to find where the two Astro devils are."

"I'm on it."

John flipped his com to engineering. "Chief, get those wings deployed I want the batteries charged as soon as possible. And double check the reactor, I want it at 100% as soon as you can," John ordered with a harsh edge to his commands.

"Its all still compact. I can't be sure of anywhere on the station that isn't being used," Jen said. They won't be able to transport onto the station.

John pulled on the helm and slowly maneuvered the *Grace* around the outside of the space station, looking for an entry port or a secondary hatch. He was fairly certain with this design that there was one on each side of the module in case of an emergency. The only question was whether it was operational after the punishment it had taken from their re-entry.

"John, I'm patching you through to Lt. Samuels from Tiger Squadron."

"Lieutenant, did your squadron make it through the gravity wave, okay?"

"Yes sir, we were out practicing joint maneuvers when the grav wavefront hit us. We are two minutes away. Sir, are you ok, did you suffer much damage when the wavefront came through? We didn't see you get back."

John gritted his teeth. "We are fine... Okay, I want you to proceed to the comm module on the space station. There is an entry airlock below what's left of the communications dish."

"Roger that."

It took a minute and thirty seconds before the squadron reached the station.

"Holy sheet the station's battered. Where's the *Versailles*?"

"They EJP'ed. Lieutenant, I need you to focus."

"Sorry sir, I see it... The hatch doesn't look too damaged. I'm preparing to go to EVA. Hold on 2 minutes while I blow the canopy." The sleek Astro Devil rounded the edge of the station. Small movement thrusters set the space fighter to synchronize its movement with the station.

John could see a slight puff as the clear plastic canopy of the Astro Devil's cockpit drifted slowly away from the fighter's fuselage. The fluoro-lit flight suit became visible as Lt. Samuels pushed off from his seat towards the station's comm maintenance hatch. After a few minutes, the lieutenant reported that the hatch was getting power but was inoperable.

John was looking for a second entrance when Lt. Samuels called over the comm, "Hey Jillaroo, give us a lift to the next hatch will ya." John was stunned to see the second fighter zip in close, while the lieutenant pushed off to catch the nose of the fighter then surf it like a wave from Malibu. Samuels had magnetized his boots to the hull, waving his arms for balance as the ship fired its maneuvering thrusters. "You'll owe me a Tequila Sunrise for this..." said Lt. Eléonore Bouchard. John could feel her smile at Samuels's antics from the cockpit.

"Huh," Samuels said.

John grimaced. He was sure Samuels didn't know if Eléonore meant a drink or a trip to the Bahamas. Both would probably suit him.

"When you two have quite finished hanging ten, I want that shield down so I can land the *Grace* on the station." Both officers chorused back over the comm, "Yes, Sir."

Lt. Samuels entered through the hatch, his voice much more subdued when it came over the comm. "It's pretty messed up in here. I've counted three dead so far. I'm passing the environment module ..."

Several agonizing minutes later the station's shields dropped, allowing the *Grace* to fly through the light curtain and land.

Before John left the bridge, he pressed the comm. "Lt. Bouchard, stay on patrol in case the station blows." Jen gave John the '*How can he be so calm?* look.'

Minutes later, John hurried through the airlock to the station and one of the consoles in the corridor. Quickly he entered his security details to bring up an internal status of the station and a staff listing.

"How many people are on board?" Jen asked as she crowed in behind him biting her bottom lip.

"Seven." John pressed the internal comm broadcast, "Station personnel, please report in."

Professor Oleman reported he was stuck in his quarters a few doors from the galley module. John had to mute his comm from all his cussing.

"Max, log on and check what you can of the station's vital systems. Jen, you've got the gravity projectors, Lt. Samuels, you check the reactor." Before John could assign tasks to the remainder of the scientists, his comm pinged him... "Admiral, is that you?" John had been using an open channel. "Yes, and you are?"

"System Specialist Rajin. We were attacked or something, there was no warning. I can't contact the others." The man's speech was stilted and faded off.

"Where are you now, Rajin?"

"Huh... I'm in the alpha reactor module trying to ... umm, stabilize it. It's not my field, but when the lights flickered off after the attack, I thought I had better check... You can't have shields ... life-support without power." Rajin said in a vague and unfocused manner.

"Stay at the reactor, help is on the way. Do you know where the other station crew are?"

"Most were working on the communications array because we've been having some problems with... it since it was deployed."

"What about the others, where would they be?"

"The Dutchman should be in the hangar bay, ... he was working on the replacement shuttle ... for the Trader system."

Damn! We just went straight through the hangar. John turned to Lt. Samuels, nodding for him to continue to the reactor, and John would check the hangar. John turned around and pulled himself toward the hanger one-handed, the other holding his tablet. Despite him trying to reconnect with Rajin through his pad as he floated through the air bridge back to the hangar, all he got was nonsensical ramblings. He commed Max, who had logged in to one of the station's console, "Max, who else is left?"

Max brought up a list of station personnel on his screen and started verbally listing names and specialties to give the rescuers an idea where they may be found, "Ah, biochemist and security specialist, Margaret Hanks-"

"What's that name?" Jen asked frowning.

"Margaret or Mags Hanks."

Jen's eyes owled with fear. "Oh my God, it can't be her! John, I have to go look for her." Jen tapped her suit vid private conference link with John. His grainy image flickered on her sleeve screen despite the interference.

"I need to find her!" Jen cried. She was already moving, and her high-pitched voice made it clear she was becoming frantic.

John was confused and anxious at Jen's instant reaction to this Mags person. Then it dawned on him:

Jen's long-lost sister was called Mags or Margaret. He couldn't remember what Jen's father's surname was because Jen took on her mother's maiden name. Trying out the name Hanks in his head to see if he could recall hearing it before; he had no luck, it was still foreign.

"Your sister?"

Jen nodded, unable to speak.

"Of course! You make a start while I-," John was speaking to air as Jen had already cut the connection.

Max shook his head in a double take at Jen's behavior but decided to pursue questioning them both when the crisis was over. He had other serious work to do.

John entered the hangar control center looking for the Dutchman. Not finding him, he searched for the light switches. Since the station had just been activated, not all the lighting had been needed nor set up yet. In the far corner of the maintenance area, lights cast eerie shadows on the wall where a small shuttle was pinned. It stood forlornly with its hood up and electrical guts floating in the air as if in the middle of a surgical operation. John braced himself against the hatch-frame then pushed off the bulkhead and floated toward the shuttle. He looked for any handholds, but in the dim light, they were impossible to see. *Thud!*

When John reached the shuttle, he gripped the edge and twisted his body as he floated straight over the top feet first. Bending his knees, he absorbed the impact when his body hit the bulkhead behind the shuttle. Grabbing the shuttle fender so he could anchor his feet to the wall, he twisted his helmet light to see into the back crevasse that was cast in shadow. Raising his visor, he kept moving around the shuttle until he heard a moan. John spotted the mechanic's leg protruding at an unnatural angle from beneath the left wheel strut. He found the Dutchman lying wedged between the wall and the strut's housing with a gash to his head seeping blood into the air. The man's leg was shattered with exposed shards of bone and spheres of blood that pooled as they floated around the drive wheel. He had to quickly get a tourniquet and compression bandage with fibrin on his leg before the blood could exsanguinate. In space, the body's blood tended to slosh around inside the skin more than on Earth.

Half in shadow, the Dutchman's Fluro overalls had an ever-increasing dark stain over his shoulder and protruding right leg where the globules splattered onto the absorbent material.

"Dutchman, can you hear me. We are going to get you out. Hold tight." The was a moan in response. John looked around for something to lever the housing off, nothing. *Damn!*

John squeezed in next to the Dutchman, bracing himself against the bulkhead then putting his feet on the housing he pushed with all his might. Nothing moved.

Damn, he thought; I need to go to the gym! It would take more than a few people to move this thing. Glancing back down at the man slowly bleeding to death, John tried again. It was futile.

Dragging himself out, he looked around for any sort of forklift or craft positioning machine, but the base was so new that none of those devices were unpacked yet. Thinking furiously at what else he could do apart from getting the *Grace* to tow it out, he had another thought while slapping his open helmet at how dumb he was. Pulling himself hand over hand to the shuttle's rear hatch, he looked for the electro-magnetic skid locks that held the shuttle to the deck. Tuning them on was common practice in space dock. Nobody wanted a ten-ton vehicle to move while it was being worked on. He chastised himself for not thinking of it first. Quickly he shut them down.

Outside the shuttle, he braced himself once again against the bulkhead and pushed the ship away. The shuttle screeched as something metallic had snagged the ship to the deck. Once clear of the remainder of the floor clamp, the ship flew across the hangar slamming into the side of the *Grace*. John gritted his teeth and took a deep breath to hold it with a prayer, he hoped he hadn't done any damage. That was all they needed to break their only means to a hospital. Geez, *this was turning out to be one hell of a day,* John thought. He carefully made his way back to the unconscious Dutchman.

♦♦♦

Training Simulators, Rams Head Station

Mags had been stuck in the Training Simulator for hours but had seemed more like days. At first, when she was thrown to the floor, she thought it was part of the sim. But when the photo laser relays for the hologram flickered and died, she knew it was something more serious.

Mags moved to the door controls. "Control this is Hanks... Control?... come in Control..., anybody..." the comm console lights faded. "Shit!!" She tried the door: nothing. Mags checked her air and battery. "Shit, and double shit!"

Resigning herself to the figures on the gauge she sat next to the door to conserve what she had. Normally backup oxygen and skin suits were available everywhere, but the module wasn't scheduled to be deployed until the

5th, so the supplies hadn't been stocked. She wasn't supposed to be in the sims.

Mags had never been good at sitting still. Her mind would churn in circles, rehashing possibilities with probabilities. Now all she could do was sit, wait and hope the others realized she was missing and come search for her, preferably before she froze to death or ran out of oxygen. She frowned in thought. *What could have caused the jolt to the station sending her to the floor?*

Once she had exhausted all the possibilities she could think of, her mind returned to the churn. Self-recrimination set her mind reeling. She thought of her stepmother and the lengths she went to, to remain the anonymous benefactor to Mag's career. She thought of her birth mother and her long-lost sister, who were never there. Mags explored every inch of the room in search of anything useful. Nothing, so she tried to sleep.

The temperature inside the sim dropped below freezing. Meanwhile, Mags started to shiver despite the warmth her suit provided. Checking the charge on her internal suit battery, there was less than fifty percent. Damn the cold, she cursed. She needed to drop the suit's heaters again as they were using too much battery. She was in a difficult position: use the batteries for heat or to pump in her oxygen. Mags went back to sleep without resolving her dilemma.

Two hours later, Mags woke; her body was shutting down. All the symptoms were there: slow breathing, drowsiness, confusion, and uncontrollable shivering. How long had it been? The possibility of dying, here and now, seemed stark and real. There was one thing to be thankful for that there was no wind to create windchill. Mags thought about crying, but it was insufferably cold.

Hours later the lights above flickered then came on. Mags knew she was groggy, from either just waking up but more likely it was from a lack of oxygen or the cold. She tried to stand but crumpled near the door. She didn't want to look at her sleeve gauge. Sleep seemed inevitable...

Chapter 21

Rams Head Station

"Admiral!! This is Lieutenant Borchard. I have two contacts in-system on a ballistic course towards the station. One frigate and the other a corvette. I'm charging my lasers, what are your orders?"

"What the hell!" John thought furiously about what to do with this new threat.

"Max, I want you to check whether we can get any shielding back up straight away!"

"Oleman, you and the scientists operate any laser weapons that are currently operational."

"John do you need me to...-" Jen started to ask before John interrupted her.

"I want you to keep searching for Mags and the other survivors! We may have to abandon the station; Bowman, you'll need to get Rajin and the Dutchman ready for evac." Jen looked relieved, despite it all.

After several agonizing minutes, Lt. Bouchard reported in. "Admiral, I have eyes-on." Her lidar and tachy scans skimming over the hull. "One of the bogies is a wreck. It's only the front third of a frigate; it looks like it was ripped to shreds. The second ship doesn't have any life signs. No running lights... just reactor leakage. It looks adrift." The Lieutenant continued to verbalize her report on the broken vessels as she closed the distance. Debris was slowly drifting away from the bulk of the two ships.

A few minutes later the *Grace* exited the Rams Head hangar bay. The fast start was a terrible way to get the *Grace* operational because it damaged the finely tuned propulsion system. John scanned the main systems and continued to quickly complete what he could of the pre-flight check in-flight. He didn't know if he could fly and shoot the heavy cannon lasers at the same time. He guessed that he would only be able to fire the HP202 missiles, which were self-guided, ship-to-ship, set-and-forget missiles. Damn, he should have waited for one of the others to join him. He had a sinking 'too late' feeling.

"Bringing up the shields," he said it aloud to nobody except the voice logger.

John steered the *Grace* on an intercept course with the second ship, the most intact one. "Lieutenant keep an eye out for a third ship, there were three chasing us."

The was a pause. "Yes, Admiral."

Suddenly as if on cue, there was a blinding flash, and the tachyon sensors went wild.

"A New contact," the Lieutenant yelled, "and it's big!"

"Max, have you got the contact?" John asked.

"Yes, I'm at the tactical station, I'm working on a fire solution." Max accessed the automated weapons targeting menus on the station's defense console.

"*Grace*, this is the *T.M.N. Aneska*, Captain Fernandez commanding."

John blew out the breath he was holding.

"Fernandez, this is a battle zone, what the hell are you doing here?!"

"Uh... Admiral Dunn sent us..."

Jason had to be crazy sending a freighter.

John switched gears, "Fernandez, we have two hostile warships inbound. I want you away from the station ASAP. By the way, welcome to Rams Head."

"Admiral, we have weapons." He sounded miffed.

"They're pea shooters compared to the frigate. Just get your ship out of here. Oh, do you have marines aboard?"

"... Yes, Captain Waters is here, Admiral."

A female voice broke in, "Admiral, I have made two flybys without a response. The intact ship looks battered," Lt. Bouchard said on an open channel.

John looked back at the tactical map and the *Aneska*.

"We seem to have an alien ship next door we need to neutralize."

"Ah, yes I see-"

There was some background clutter noise. "Admiral, Captain Waters here."

"Captain, assemble your men, suit up with battle gear, full amour."

John could hear the marine Captain start barking orders to his squad over the comm.

"Captain Fernandez, I presume you have SAR teams aboard?"

"Yes, sir," Fernandez responded.

"The station has taken a beating but be aware, the aliens may come back online any minute."

"Yes, sir, shuttle 01 is on its way. My helm has the EJP button primed."

John shook his head, they would be dead before they could press it. He made a note to commend their bravery when he got back, and to chastise Jason for sending them.

A small shuttle detached from the hull of the freighter and headed towards the space station.

John moved the *Grace* to dock with the freighter.

The small airlock in the back, aired-up to let the marines aboard. It reminded John that the Merchant ships weren't entirely defenseless. They had small shields around the engines and command modules with a detachable defense weapons package bolted to the mid-frame. There was a troop aboard who were trained to repel boarders.

"Captain Waters, it's good to see you," John said as he returned the man's salute when he entered through *Grace's* airlock.

"This is a whole new species, so we don't know what to expect." John looked at the Marine to gauge his reaction to the implied unknown risks.

The heavyset man bristled with weapons, grenades, and armor. He stood confident and self-assured. "We need to get moving, in case the ship starts waking up."

John nodded at the truth of it. "Keep your comms open and locators active. We'll pull you out if there's trouble." Capt. Waters nodded and headed back through the corridor towards the airlock.

Over the open channel, John heard Max's sprightly voice, "Look at that large gun barrel protruding out of the main turret. Do you think they are compensating?"

Capt. Waters coughed, hiding a smirk.

"Focus, Max," John said with quiet authority. "Captain, I would like to come with you. However, I need to remain in command of *Grace* in case they power up and try to run. I won't let them leave here alive." John said with concern.

The Marine Captain stood frozen, processing what John just said. If the aliens started up their ship, the Admiral was, if necessary, going to blow the ship, with them on it. With an almost imperceptible nod, Waters moved to join his squad.

Waters stood with his men inside the entryway to the *Grace*. The boarding party checked each other's kit a second time. John was relieved that they didn't look outwardly daunted at the prospect of taking an unknown alien ship.

John brought up Capt. Water's service record on his personal HUD in his glasses. Although the marine had completed the necessary training for boarding actions, he was by no means an expert. At least some of his team had seen combat during the battle for Earth. John could see the man, in a private moment, take a deep breath at his heavy responsibility.

Without further hesitation, he followed his men through the inner hatch to evacuate the air.

"Max, any other contacts before we enter the beast?"

"No, the board is clear."

John steered the *Grace* near what looked like an external airlock in the mid-ship.

Sitting at the helm, John switched to Grace's stern cameras. He clicked on the image of the alien airlock through his side targeting camera used for lining up airlocks. On the screen in four places, crosshairs appeared so *Grace's* autopilot could reference it for station keeping with the alien vessel.

A large muscled marine moved to *Grace's* external hatch controls. Once the rear airlock had depressurized, he opened the outer door, aimed two feet from the alien airlock and fired the super strong magneto grapples. The thin wire would allow the marines to shimmy along the cable to board the other ship. The grapples were a low-tech last resort for ship-to-ship transfers where the airlock was damaged.

John walked up behind the marine Captain to spot him through the peep window, "Normally I'd transport you into the hangar bay, but that doesn't look operational right now," John said as he and Captain Waters watched the first of his squad stand on the hull of the alien craft held by their magnetized boots.

"If you can't open the hatch...?" John asked.

"Joe brought some explosives."

John concentrated on the Captain. "I need you to look for a jump drive."

Minutes later, it was the Marine Captain's turn to rappel the guide wire between the ships.

Max looked through the station window and spied a glint of reflected light that he suspected was a heavily armored man as he crossed to the other ship. "John, remind me why we don't send the ship to Titan, where we have lots of guns?"

"Max, they jumped here."

"The other ship doesn't look too good. If the aliens did jump, they're not very good at it. Could their drive still work?"

John thought Max was right. *If they had jump drives, why did they botch coming here?* Then it occurred to him. *They probably hitched a ride with us... in the gravity bubble or its wake.*

John pursed his lips. "Maybe... I'm not taking the risk. If they escape, it's another deadly species that knows where we live."

Max stared at the *Grace* and realized his friend John had become an Admiral. He had come to trust John's leadership, but was his assessment correct? The risk seemed excessive for the boarding team and small for the Titan capture group. There were rumors that John was losing it. Giving up Pete's brain, then always having the stinky Lizard Rezulin hanging around. Max clenched his fists. He hated the Lizards as much as the next guy.

John flew the *Grace* toward the hollow in the alien ship's hull that he suspected was a hangar bay. He was relieved that the ship's shields were still not active and there seemed to be no sign of charging weapons. Even the atmospheric light curtain that held the air in within the hangar bay was down. John worried about auto defense weapons in the bay itself if he were to land. It would be better the marines checked it out on the inside first.

John swiped his screen that displayed the comm board and turned onto the Marine's comm channel. The speakers in *Grace's* bridge came alive as John brought up the live suit feed on Captain Water's helmet.

♦♦♦

Outside Midship Hatch, Gnoll Frigate

Sam floated downside up in zero-G as she examined the alien vessel's hatch controls. The skinsuit couldn't hide her solid muscular frame, the product of a military career of harsh physical conditioning. She knew what functionality should be there on the hatch. She had studied both the Squishy and Lizard hatch controls in her training for the Electronics Specialist (ES1) role in the squad; she was the hatch breaker. She set her suit to station-keeping mode, preventing her from floating away while she worked. Gently she pushed aside the thick metal cover that protected the external hatch controls. The Captain had given Corporal Caza, the unit's beef pounder, the ok to use the electro-crow-bar to pull off the outer hatch covering. Sam shook her head as she spied some motion sensors attached to the hull nearby. *I guess they know we're coming now.*

Captain Waters voice was calm despite the tense situation. He reminded each team of their objectives. "Bravo team, you will work your way to the stern and secure the engine and reactor rooms. Alpha team is with me, we'll head for the bridge. Focus and listen to your team leaders, that includes you Caza," who had lost interest and was staring up the length of the hull.

Admittedly, it was a rare thing one could say they stood and gazed out upon the hull of an alien warship just before a boarding action entry.

Waters directed his next comments to the team noncoms on a private channel. "Stay in contact, minimum teams of two. Look out for any unusual drive systems that can make jumps like ours."

"But we've never seen our own drive, how would we know what it looks like," the Bravo Squad Leader complained.

"I know, I know ... Admiral, can you give us an idea of what this jump drive thing should look like?"

"The drive itself can be anything from the size of a large refrigerator or bigger." John could hear the squad members groan in the background.

"Just do your best! If you think you have something, we'll get the Admiral on the vid feed," the Captain replied conscious that the Admiral could hear them complain like babies, just like he could.

The door mechanism was protected but didn't stand a chance against Sam's computer hacking software. Slowly the hatch popped inward at her touch. It was another indicator that the standard of computer tech in the galaxy was low. For an external hatch on a warship, it should have had decent encryption to stop just the sort of thing they were doing, unauthorized entry.

Sam put away her gear as Caza entered, prying the actuators on the hatch with the crowbar. The sticky airlock popped open giving Caza access followed by Bravo squad. Pressing the large red button next to the inner door caused the outer hatch to close automatically before air filled the airlock.

Bracing themselves on the walls of the airlock, barrel torchlights on, stun guns at the ready. Slowly the inner hatch swung open; Caza pushed off like a bullet through the zero-g inner hatch. The man dropped like a stone to the deck when he passed the threshold. Two men behind him tumbled on top.

Sam spied another sequence of icons above the door loosely translated to "Warning: Watch your step, gravity." They had gravity plates under the deck. Holding back a smile, she checked the corridor with her M40 taser hybrid automatic without going out into the corridor.

Captain Waters shook his head and made a silent prayer for all his men as Bravo team got to their feet and made their way down and around the corner toward the stern of the ship. Gravity was like Earth's. Looking through the faceplates of his reduced Alpha squad, Waters tried to gauge their fear levels. Traipsing through an alien ship in the torchlit dark was bound to set off fear reactions, so he started directing his team onward, heading for the bow of the ship to get them busy. Waters then readjusted his HUD to limit each solders vitals to the side and faded it so as not restrict his close quarter fighting vision.

John switched channels to contact the space station.

"Max how's it going... Are there any lasers online?"

"John, we've only managed to get two beamers up and running, both of them are on the side facing away from the alien ships. Lieutenant Samuels has been able to remove the fluctuations in the reactor core, so he's now attempting to shunt it through to the shields. On the other matter, we are still missing two crew."

"Okay, understood... If you can't get the enemy facing lasers online soon, we'll try to rotate the station to bring the active lasers on target. Keep at it, *Grace* out."

The bridge of the *Aneska* appeared on John's HUD. "Capt. Fernandez, how is the SAR proceeding?"

"Admiral, we've transferred the sickest of the survivors to the *Aneska*. The Professor is spitting chips, he wants a report on what caused the attack. I told him that enemy ships are nearby. That seemed to quieten him. He's headed to the main control room."

John sighed at the Professor's justifiable anger. Something to deal with later.

"Ok, thanks."

"We'll jump as soon as we have a confirmed count unless you want us to wait till the boarding action has been completed?"

"Hold, I'll see how the boarding party is going."

John switched back to the combat channels used by the Marines. "We have found quite a few dead aliens. They look like different species. The condition of some of them... Well, I don't think the damage was all from popping through n-space. There are quite a few with old wounds and scarred limbs. Many have lost an appendage altogether. These aliens are no stranger to violence."

"Acknowledged."

"Contact! Contact!" A loud bang could be heard.

"Bravo? Alpha Actual, Bravo report!"

"Captain, we've got ... coming outa the walls."

"Colin, Report!"

Then a calmer voice came on "Bravo Sgt. Hill, Alpha Actual we have contact! Small arms and laser fire! Taser bullets are effective. The team leader has been wounded. I'm taking command of Bravo."

"Alpha Actual. Confirmed Sgt. Hill is the new Bravo lead." Waters updated the tactical response screen. At the same time, he checked Colin's health status. There were two red and three green lights below his picture.

Captain Waters switched channels to a private channel within the Alpha team.

"Alpha team, sound off your taser bullets and flashbang munitions."

Waters cringed at the small supply of ordnance their squad carried: they would have to make it count.

Slowly they forced their way through the ship; Alpha team stunned any being they came across, giving them no quarter. They were luckier than Bravo team. Although the distance from the hatch to engineering was not as far as midship to the bridge, they had a lot more armed resistance on their route. The Captain could hear dull fighting in the background through his comm. It had progressed from small arms to explosives. He held his breath when he saw on his HUD Bravo team had their first casualty, Pvt Gordon. Water's filed it away for when there was time. He did notice the Admirals drawn breath over the comm when the flatline showed on his HUD.

Picking their way forward, Alpha Team leapfrogged as they covered each other's movements. The ship's lights suddenly flared on strongly after momentary flickering since they had boarded the vessel. Something or someone was fixing the power. The boarding team's faceplates immediately adjusted to the brightness.

"*Grace*, Alpha Actual, we are picking up an energy reading buildup in the ship."

"Alpha Actual, *Grace,* that's affirmative, we have lights on over here."

John looked at Max on the vid connection, the worry evident in his eyes. "Max, get the station turned now."

John split his attention to powering up the laser guns and missile racks on the *Grace*.

Aboard the Gnoll frigate, small Ferret like people rushed towards Alpha Team carrying weapons of a sort only to be cut down ruthlessly by taser fire. Two of the Ferrets froze mid-stride with fur standing on end like an electrified porcupine. Once they were hit by a taser bullet, they spasmed then scrunched, dropped to the deck and vomited. Captain Waters could see them breathing hard as they slipped unconscious.

An explosion ripped through the compartment bulkhead knocking the nearby troopers from their feet. Corpl. Tyler, on point, landed with a smack, cracking his faceplate. The man visibly paled at the jagged line on his helmet. He knew the risks of breathing in the alien atmosphere. Frantically he reached for the tape on his belt to cover the cracks.

Waters grabbed the back panel of Tyler's suit then dragged him out of the line of fire. A second Marine joined them, brushing away Tyler's ineffectual attempts at fixing his own helmet. She deliberately pulled her tape, winding it over the crack and around his helmet. She then smacked his helmet and gave him the thumbs-up-query? Tyler looked down at his sleeve, checking the pressure and gave a reluctant thumbs-up back to Josie, who smiled.

Captain Waters crept past just as two marines dived forward behind a large hose-like device. Breathing hard, he peeked over the hose housing then after a split decision jumped up into a running crouch. He dashed forward, aiming his weapon at the corners and barriers.

Snatching a look at the hose object with a fridge-sized housing, he turned on his comm.

Breathing hard, he said, "Admiral, what about that?"

"Captain, I need a better look."

Waters sighed, then stuck his head out in the corridor. He didn't see the housing. Instead, there was a scarred ferret pointing a gun at his face from thirty feet away.

Before he had time to react, Josie pulled him back with such force he hit the wall behind the bulkhead with a thud.

A fireball whizzed past their cover were Waters was a second ago. Waters let out a gasp. "Thanks, JJ!"

Josie stared meaningfully at the Capt. for a microsecond before standing and firing her weapon.

Waters shook his head at his carelessness, then ground his teeth and timed it with Josie, he leaned out with his weapon. His carbine unleashed a staccato of bullets before tasering an exposed bear-like creature. He wondered what had happened to the scarred Ferret. Josie stepped sideways and ran past him spraying controlled bursts of gunfire with Tyler at her heels shooting taser bullets. An explosion ripped through the ceiling near him throwing Waters to the deck. Breathing heavily, he struggled to a kneeling position as loose conduit and plastics fell on and around him.

Two more explosions behind Waters rocked the deck as debris and wall paneling fell, striking the remaining troopers as they jumped for cover.

Loud alien screams of unintelligible threats directed at the Humans were punctuated by bursts of staccato fire.

Waters signaled one of his men to lob a nine-count flashbang deep behind the skirmish line. The man stood, threw the grenade, then crouched back under cover to wait until the ninth deafening bang with its blinding flash echoed down the narrow corridor.

"Go. Go. Go!"

The marines jumped up, for good or ill, didn't wait for the smoke to clear. They charged down the hall, firing as they went, grim animalistic snarls escaped their mouths.

◆◆◆

John could hear intense fighting through the comm and knew he would have sleepless nights over it. The screams and deafening staccato barks from the Marines' weapons and the crew of the alien warship chilled him to the bone. Wild in nature, it reminded him of his time as a Marine patrolling the Burmese jungle back in the '90s.

Several more life signs blinked red. John fought the urge to look away. More deaths on his conscience. He couldn't look away from his screen.

Chapter 22

Bridge, Gnoll Frigate *Wild Roar*

Lord Saga's ship swerved moments before the enormous gravity wave struck, destroying the starboard shields and battering the crystalline bonded metallic armor of the outer hull. On the bridge, all but the Lordling were thrown from their stations.

There was a stunned silence as the crew returned to their places.

"What happened? Report!?" Saga was fuming.

"Lord Volund's ship has been destroyed."

"No transponders from *Light Bringer*?"

"No. What's left of *Tallos the Blade* is scattered. I'm picking up four different transponder readings. All four pieces of the hull on separate ballistic courses. The front third of the ship is missing just before the main gun emplacement."

The operations officer had to yell over the multiple alarms throughout the ship. "Repair crews are being sent to deal with hull breaches on 2nd and 4th decks, starboard side. Engineering crews are attempting to access the shield projectors. We have reports of structural damage midship which has bent the forward missile tracks. Racks three and four are unable to reload because the bulkhead took a beating there. Forward and starboard shields are currently off-line."

"Any sign of the little ship?"

"No, Master."

Lord Saga paced back and forth like a caged creature. Blood dripped around her claw as she clutched her wrist after it had been damaged in the buffeting. "They dove into the star's gravity well. Did they cause this deliberately?" she said aloud. *Of course, they did.*

"That is an unknown master. In the past, we crossed paths with religious zealots that committed suicide when their beliefs were questioned. Although this attitude is extreme, it's not unheard of. It is common knowledge that ships cannot enter or leave subspace near a star, it would be ripped apart."

Lord Saga stiffened at the obvious, confirming her fears. She snapped her head around to face the little alien and wondered briefly if the furry officer's twitches were a sign of disrespect or fear.

"I want you to scour this region for any sign of my brother and that little ship, and I mean scan every molecule." Lord Saga turned and left the bridge, dismissing the operations officer to get on with his work.

Once the Gnoll Lord had left, the crew sagged and gawped at each other. *None had experienced their Lord acting so... restrained. What did it mean?* She was normally like a switch that flicked her behavior from one extreme to the other. Surely this change in her meant certain death if one didn't comply immediately.

When Lord Saga reached her cabin, she calmly entered and locked the door. After a pregnant pause, she bellowed until her throat was hoarse. Anger seethed through her like molten lava, blistering her raw emotions. Every piece of furniture was butchered beyond recognition.

Chapter 23

Gnoll Frigate Light Bringer, Rams Head

Captain Waters looked down at the bloodied mess at his feet. They had made it to the bridge. He had to give the aliens credit, they had been persistent if not successful in their defense. What he could only assume was the Captain, lay stunned behind the shattered environmental controls. It had taken five taser bullets to take him down. Each one could knock out a rhino. Sparks still flew from the broken pieces of console nearby.

Bravo team had been equally challenged. They had encountered heavy resistance in a dozen different areas on the ship. Waters figured there were at least thirteen different species aboard this one warship. The high number meant that these people were either well traveled or they were highly aggressive. Given the way they fought on the ship, especially the furry lion-looking creature on the bridge, he had no doubts that aggression was their modus operandi.

When the warship's hangar bay was cleared of debris, John docked the *Grace*. Outside the hatch, he saw a few smaller craft that looked like scooters. John shook his head at what looked like a Star Wars air bike. He put his skin suit facemask on then proceeded over to the access hatch of the much larger ship.

"Captain Walters?" The nearest marine pointed further in. When he found the Captain, John stepped in close to personalize their conversation. "Ray, I'm sorry for the loss of your men. Our only other choice would have been to blow the alien ship without getting any intel. What we'll learn here from them," he said, pointing at one of the dead aliens, "could save millions back on Earth. If these aliens find Earth before we are ready..." John let the meaning hang in the air. "Please give my thanks to the men for the good work they did today."

Ray nodded.

Suddenly a small hamster-sized creature jumped off the ceiling with its claws extended toward John's head. John caught it in his peripheral vision and slapped the creature aside. The creature squealed as it struck the deck. John lifted his mag boot intending to stamp on it as if it were vermin but stopped mid stamp. The alien creature had raised all eight of its paws in surrender. Capt. Waters stood aghast, his face mirroring that of the Admiral.

"Geez, that thing's sentient."

The little alien glared at one Human then the other.

"Dawson!" Ray yelled, "Roundup, this little fellow and put him with the rest of the crew."

"Yes, sir. Ahh, Captain, I don't speak alien, how do I..."

"Put a gun in his face and point in the right direction."

Little hamster braced itself, preparing to make a dash for the hatch, but John knelt and looked at it straight in the six eyes as he pointed towards the makeshift holding cell.

John got the distinct impression that the little fellow wasn't usually spoken to directly, like an 18th-century kitchen boy who went about his business and was never seen by the master or mistress of the house.

News of the hamster spider attack and the way the Admiral dealt with the little alien broke the tension that had built up over their boarding action. Some marines didn't believe the rumors of John's rise to fame, fighting aliens on freighters with nothing more than a silo class ship and large *cojones*. Doubters were soon jeered down.

Captain Waters and his two teams had captured 24 aliens with the loss of two marines and five wounded. Admittedly the Humans were all in armor. They had, however, still considered themselves extremely lucky. He was pleased that Bravo team had come across a large brig not far from the hangar. The size of the brig gave the marines a dark feeling about the need for such a room. Ray ordered all the aliens moved to it.

Marine search teams made their way through the ship flushing out any stragglers; in the process, they discovered what looked like a medical bay. With the help of some of the station scientists, they set up a triage for the wounded aliens by separating them from the healthier looking crew.

One of four eight-armed biobeds started pulsing when the marines placed one of the wounded aliens on it. The console lit up with strange writing.

Corpl. Tyler moved toward the console and started pushing buttons at random.

"Do you know what you're doing," Josie said from behind.

"Nope."

Josie shook her head then turned toward the wounded crew catching their attention then back at Tyler and nodded.

An older Ferret with greying fur shuffled forward, shaking his head in what Josie assumed was disgust.

"Corp, we got a medic in the crew."

"Good, cause I think this damn thing's broken. Nothing on it works."

"Just let the Ferret do it." Josie watched as Tyler shrugged.

The old Ferret winced as he touched the controls with his own broken arm. He struggled to operate the medical bed controls. They learned from his actions on how to run the machine's basic diagnostic and treatment programs. The spidery arms flicked in and over the patient with speedy *Grace* as it treated the wounded furry person. The sick and wounded looking aliens were all transferred to the medical area under guard where the older Ferret continued running the medical beds. When the large cat was escorted to the Med-bay, the other aliens were reluctant to receive treatment until they started on what they assumed was the Captain first. Captain Waters just shrugged at their weird sense of priorities. It was only when it looked like two of the crew were at death's door that Ray stepped in, placing a gun to the old Ferret's head ordering him to fix the other two seriously wounded aliens first. The Big Cat sat regarding the Human's behavior with what seemed like indifference, eventually waving his paw to give his crew permission.

Although the Gnoll sat in the corner, his feline body projected power and authority. Ray, confronting the Cat as he did, made their confrontation personal. Humans were no strangers to lord and servant relationships. History was littered with it. Ray himself had researched his family tree to discover to his surprise some ties to minor Irish nobility *and* convicts. He then considered the interaction between the alien beings. It had elements of lord and commoner, or master and slave. The feline was in no immediately obvious medical danger, and so it could wait. However, Ray knew then he'd made a dangerous enemy that day. He suspected that the Cat, like Earth lions, did not give up their territory without a fight.

Chapter 24

Rams head Space Station

John arrived at the station control center to manage the situation. The *Aneska* was preparing to jump back to Sol.

After forty-eight hours straight on-duty, Lieutenant Bouchard struggled to keep her yawn in.

John turned to each Lieutenant. "You both have done an outstanding job today. Bouchard, go get some sack time. Samuels, I'll need you to pull another shift patrolling the system. The sensors on the station are still playing up." John realized that they both worked well together and wondered if there was something more between them. Could this be a problem? In the end, he put that thought aside.

"Sir, if I may, I'd like to keep searching for the last missing scientist?" said Bouchard.

"Very well."

Margaret, or Mags as Jen called her, had still not been found. Jen was getting desperate, jumping at any possibility, and figuratively biting people's heads off.

John turned to the other two men in the center. "Max, Professor Oleman," his two next senior officers aside from Jen, "what's the situation here?" Prof. Oleman straightened his shoulders.

"We have accounted for all except Miss Hanks; Hickman is checking the waste compactor."

John could feel Jen scowl behind him.

The three walked over to the operations table where a replica mini-holo of the station slowly rotated.

"What's that there?" John said as he pointed to a dulled-out area.

"It's the ancillary modules. Hanks wouldn't be there, we haven't deployed that area yet." Oleman then gave a quick look over at Jen, who was making her way towards the table.

Gulping, looking over at the door, he said, "I'll go and search that area." He turned and ran from the room.

John frowned at the back of the quickly disappearing man. "They're trying their best, Jen."

Max cringed at John's tepid reprimand knowing Jen's state of mind. Max turned and looked out the large portal windows avoiding the inevitable.

Jen turned on John, her eyes ablaze. "They can be lazy on their own time, not mine ... or Mag's!"

"You're right. They can sleep later," John said, backing down as he saw her drawing breath to express more views. Not that she was wrong.

Max looked at his two friends. "I'll make sure Oleman searches everywhere," he said as he left the room.

Max and Prof. Oleman entered the latest 6X module configuration that was attached to the main station structure. The ancillary modules were attached to each axis of the six-way junction. Three of the modules were still ultra-compressed and had yet to be inflated. A mouse couldn't fit in there. That left the remaining two that were inflated.

Oleman checked the status of each; The first had no life support. The second module, the simulators, had limited life support. The two men donned enviro skin suits to search through the inflated modules because the status showed the modules were colder than a freezer inside.

Max's goggles darkened briefly as the junction lights started to flicker on. Main reactor power was being rerouted to the environment and life support processes.

Professor Oleman stood before the second add-on module at the end of the corridor. There were lights on the door entry. He started punching the buttons furiously, quickly moving through the security menus. "This has been unlocked and opened since yesterday morning," he said while staring at the controls.

"You didn't know?" Max was incredulous.

The man glanced at Max and shrugged. Max could feel his blood pressure rising.

"The module was not scheduled to be initialized and opened till after the second reactor was brought online. Whoever it was, they'd used emergency power to start it up."

"What's in there?" Max balled his hands into fists. The man brought up his work schedule on his datapad ... "See," he said, showing Max.

"That other date there... why is it flashing?"

Max watched the man stare at the flashing date of two days before. Frowning he tapped a few controls ... and scrolled through some menus. Max could tell he was fishing. He didn't know, and he was supposed to be the

Administrator and deployment Professor. Max shook his head, they were wasting time.

"What's in there," Max asked, trying to hold his breathing steady.

"Um, it's the brig, there is an armory and some administration with storage. Non-essentials only at startup."

Max closed in to view the console... *Security Module, Brig, Armory, Admin, Training Simulators.* Mags was a specialist in security. It was the first time Max felt like seriously hurting the man.

"The door's stuck." Oleman kept pressing the open button to a flat off key beep, signaling an environmental error.

"Doesn't the door access to the main station have a safety to stop cold air or hard vacuum coming in?"

"Yes, to protect us. The temperature in there is -10 degrees Celsius." The Professor stared at the locks.

"Well turn the damn locks off."

Max could see the Professor was taken aback by his outburst. Oleman seemed to think he was the least threatening of the Command Team on the station. Max knew Commander Gale made his legs go rubbery whenever she looked at him. The Admiral, well he could skin you alive if tested. Max was more devious, computers were his weapons of choice. But right now, he was furious for Jen; it was her little sister in trouble.

"The rerouted power will start to heat the room."

"Yeah, but how long will that take?"

Once again, Oleman shrugged. "A couple of hours."

Max hit him in the face. The man staggered against the wall with a cry, then ran off muttering about by-laws and courts.

Max rubbed his sore hand, then pulled out his pad. He used his Admin account to dive into the station infrastructure, drilling down to the door sensor to reset the default setup. To trick it to thinking anything above -270 degrees was within the normal range.

He hoped these were the only doors that were exposed to that sort of temperature because it might just cause a ... serious problem. Holding his breath, he selected to *execute.*

Suddenly the gravity plating turned off, and Max started to float. Three minutes later, the door slid open, and a chill of frosty air passed over him as it poured out of the opening. Max rushed into the ice box. A small figure huddled frozen stuck next to the door, through her faceplate her eyes were closed, lips purple. Kneeling, he pulled her forward and broke the ice holding her frozen to the wall. Carefully he lifted her lithe body and floated her back down the corridor to the warmer air and the six-way junction.

Chapter 25

Admin Control, Rams Head Station

Jen brushed her hair aside. Zero-G was damned annoying sometimes. When Max had commed her that two support modules had been turned on, she had mixed feelings. It was the biggest lead they'd had yet. She felt sure that Mags was in there... they'd searched everywhere else. She hurried toward the '6X' junction.

Max's second comm made her fly into the bulkhead. Mags had been found, but her air had almost run out. The environmental unit had gone offline when the grav wave hit the station.

Jen felt her gut twist. *No, not hypoxia please... her organs would shut down, she could become brain dead, a vegetable!*

When Jen reached them, Max had changed Mag's suit battery and was floating her to the center of the '6X' junction.

"John is teleporting her to the *Aneska* med bay," Max said. "We need to center her at the '6X' where there's enough room he can target her without taking some of the station with her."

Not long ago, Jen had laughed at John's poor targeting skills with the jump drive, but now, biting her bottom lip, she wished John was accurate. Jen helped steady Mags as she floated. *Just this once.* Minutes later Mags disappeared from the '6X' junction.

Jen called the *Aneska*. "Have you got her?!"

"Huh. Who sir?" the comm voice sounded confused.

"Put me through to your med area. Now!"

"Yes, Sir."

"Medical?!" Jen screamed.

"We've got her. We're hooking her up to the monitors now, and we'll begin warming her shortly."

Jen let out her breath then pushed off from the walls to float toward the hangar bay where the *Grace* was docked.

John had expected Jen to need a ride to the *Aneska*, so he prepared the *Grace* for immediate departure. As soon as she had closed the hatch, John cut the umbilical's, released the clamps and fired the maneuvering thrusters.

Jen made it to the Graces' bridge and sat down. A frown framed her face.

"Jen, I'm sure she'll be ok."

"She's there because of us, John. Max said the life support system in the module she was in was almost non-existent. *We* did that to her."

John had no reply. The fusion reactor had shut off all ancillary module connections when the failsafe was tripped by the grav wave. Normally those modules would have had a battery backup, but the energy collector panels for the module hadn't yet been deployed, so it had no time to charge the local batteries. Of course, it failed.

"There were a lot of things that went wrong for it to get to here," John said, waving his hand indicating everything.

"What ... your insatiable appetite for risking us all? Or was it the whole macho crap want to be the first to transport near a bloody star!!" Jen glowered at him.

John sat there, gobsmacked. *Did she really blame him for this?*

Ten minutes later, John docked with the *Aneska*. Jen left the *Grace* alone.

◆◆◆

Med Bay, *T.M.N. Aneska*

"Mags, wake up. Mags..." the voice sounded so familiar, but she couldn't place it, a female voice.

"Mags its Jen."

A doctor who stood by the monitor turned, "She's pretty dosed up. It'll be a lucky thing if she hears you."

...

"Jen?" Mags said, frowning. Mags' eyes strayed around the room. Finding nobody, but monitors and their incessant beeping. She slipped back under before she could make sense of anything.

...

"Mags, can you hear me?" said a second deeper voice, a male voice...

"She's waking..." there was relief in the tone.

"Mags, can you follow my fingers as I wave them." Mags did. "I think you're very lucky. If Max and Oleman hadn't found you when they did, another ten minutes, and I think you would have suffered brain damage or worse."

Mags focused on the man with the stethoscope.

She looked around not recognizing the room. She knew she had been all over the station, and this room wasn't there. The room looked a lot like the sick bay on the *Aneska*. But that couldn't be right, the freighter was in Sol going to the colonies soon.

"Where am I?"

"Aboard the *Aneska*."

"Artie?"

The Young officer came into her line of view. "Hey, kiddo. Good to see you're back in the land of the living." Artie held her hand.

The doctor stepped forward. "Some people would like to speak to you, but they'll have to do that when you're transferred back to Rams Head Medical. You're past the critical stage. They can take care of you, we need to get back to Earth. Others have not been so fortunate." The doctor nodded to Artie.

"What? What others?"

"There was an accident, the *Grace* jumped from deep in a gravity well and materialized near the station. It caused a massive gravity wave," he explained.

"That's what knocked me to the floor and stuck the door shut. Damn! Who's the dumbass that nearly killed me."

Artie smiled. "I'm sure the Admiral would like to hear your feedback."

Mags' eyes widened. "The Admiral? He was..."

Artie's smile widened. "Yes, he and Commander Gale have been in several times to check on you."

A man pushing a wheelchair entered the room.

"Ah, here's your ride. Now take it easy for a few days. It was a close call before your organs started to shut down. Give them time to recuperate."

Mags nodded as she transferred to the wheelchair. "Thank you, doctor."

"You're welcome. Good luck... especially with the Admiral," he said with a smirk.

Artie leaned down and kissed her cheek. "Take care, Kiddo. *Aneska's* pulling out, so I got to go."

It was good to see Artie again, she thought as she watched him leave. Although the kiss was a surprise. She was not sure how she felt about that.

♦ ♦ ♦

Mess, Rams Head Station

Mags sat in the station galley on a plastic bolt down bench. Her arms crossed as she glared across the room at her sister Jen. The two of them had been at it, arguing since the breakfast shift finished leaving them alone.

"So, you're telling me that the virtual sim broke just as you returned here in the *Grace*. Which was when the gravity wave struck. The same wave that cut the power and locked me in. Are you're saying you caused the gravity wave?" Mags demanded.

Jen didn't answer.

"Damn, you nearly killed me! I haven't seen you in like twenty years, and the first thing you do is nearly kill me."

"We didn't mean it, we were being shot at. Besides ..." Jen's voice trailed off without force.

Mags eyes narrowed. Jen looked offended as if she thought she had locked her in personally.

Mags started half-heartedly, "You didn't have your comm. T.N. policy..."

Oh, for God's sake. Mags couldn't believe it, *she's talking like some damn lawyer.* "T.N. policy, blah, blah."

Mags was livid; she stood with her face mere inches from Jen.

"T.N. policy is there to keep you safe," Jen countered weakly, her eyes cast downward.

Mags tossed her hair back and stared at her big sister in disbelief. "You know what you can do with your policy. You can shove it ..."

Just then John entered the room, surprise wrinkling his face at the chill between the two women. Mags glanced at him and frowned. She couldn't hide her distaste by association.

It shouldn't have surprised Mags that John saw the distaste between them plain as day, that Mags hated her sister. His eyes narrowed as Mags turned back to her sibling.

John turned to Jen and sucked in a breath. There were tears and what looked like a small red handprint on Jen's cheek. She wouldn't look at him.

"What the hell are you doing out here, Jen?" Mags said harshly.

"I could ask you exactly the same question!" Jen replied in a stammer, hand raised to her throbbing cheek. "I have so many questions..." Jen started, but Mags had had enough. She raised her hand in a stop signal right in front of Jen's face, cutting her off.

"I have nothing to say to you!"

"But ..."

Mags stormed out of the room, her face tight with grim determination. Of all the places to meet Jen, it would have to be out here where she was stuck and unable to leave. She had run through every conceivable scenario of their meeting as it was a recurring nightmare since she was eight. In her mind, she had fought those demons' countless times as she grew up. What she would say and do to the sister that had abandoned her. She had been left to the wolves! Her new mother had become a shopaholic, and her father, well she couldn't think about her father without raising painful memories of assault, sarcasm, and a long history of apathetic alcoholism.

John stood there a witness to a string of emotions that flashed across Jen's face. Tearstains blemished her pretty red cheeks as she watched her sister escape from the room.

Was that a handprint? John ground his teeth.

The last few days had been overwhelming for her, the tense space battle, the SAR and now this. John could almost feel her heart being crushed as she stood alone in the room. Walking up to comfort her, she looked at him in startled recognition, her lips pursed as her eyes lit with angry fire. She abruptly turned her face to wipe her tears. Purposefully she walked from the room with her arms clutched around herself defensively, looking straight ahead.

Just then Max walked into the room passing Jen in the doorway. When she ignored him, he turned a startled face to John. "Just don't ask," John said pre-emptively.

Max couldn't hide his concern but kept quiet all the same.

John walked to the window and spied the alien warship floating nearby. Max followed to stand in silence.

"I want to examine this new ship with a fine-tooth comb. We need to find out if they're being tracked before any of their friends turn up. The quick, cursory look that Waters' team did, didn't reveal any obvious jump drive or tracker, but we need to be sure if they use one or not."

"You want to take it to Sol?"

"No, there's enough chaos there with the Lizard ships. We need more people out here anyway! I thought we had lots of time, now I'm not so sure. *Three* ships were chasing us, only two are here."

The two stared quietly at the slowly rotating ship, as the ugly main gun came into view. "I had hoped to ease into this, scope out a couple of species, and pick one to focus on. With them showing up here. It changes things."

"But we brought them with us through the teleport, didn't we?"

John turned to Max. "We can't be 100% certain."

"No, but pretty certain."

"Would you risk it? The whole of humanity? Even if it was only one percent, the risk is too great. We need to find out."

John turned back to the window. They needed intel on this new threat, and quickly. It wasn't just because of the powerful gun which was now in full view, it was because thirteen different species made up the crew. They were obviously dangerous, but they also appeared organized and warlike.

"I want to take some pictures of the Captain and the crew with me to see if our friends know any of the species." John saw Max do a double take at 'our friends.' "I mean the Lizards and the Squishys." John could see Max wouldn't trust either to be called friends.

"I'll just be a few hours to *get the ball rolling*. Max, I want you to keep an eye on Jen, it seems her sister *knocked her for a six*."

Max looked at John quizzically.

John laughed, the gravel in his voice had a slight edge to it. "I've been learning Australian cricket expressions."

Max laughed. "Good luck trying to understand the Aussie woman's psyche." Both friends had in the past picked on Jen and her quirky Australianisms.

Chapter 26

Bridge, *T.N. Grace* - Outskirts of Sol System

"Transitioning into normal space." John pushed the execute button. A sudden change in pitch from *Grace's* reactors was the only indication that the high energy fields that surrounded the ship in subspace were released.

"Scans clearing." The *Grace* linked into a nearby signal booster.

John cleared the reactor and the A-Drive energy capacitors. He secured the ship for normal inter-solar operations. He was out beyond the Oort cloud and had to slow to pass through the asteroid field. On his comm panel, a red-flagged comm message blinked steadily.

"Jason?" John responded after making a comm connection. The priority message had started making incessant pinging noises.

Jason's tense face appeared on-screen. "John, what happened, the *Versailles* made an emergency jump. Well, what was left of it made the jump. I'm sorry, but we couldn't send you much help." John could hear the sad, tense resignation in his voice.

"It's okay, Jason, I understand." Silence. John couldn't admonish his friend for sending the *Aneska* into a battle zone. "We lost nine people. Five scientists from the Rams Head station and two marines from the *Aneska*. The station is secure. However, I'm not sure for how long. I've thought about whether we should leave it there or move it. How did the *Versailles* fair?" John braced himself for the bad news.

"Of the 27 crew, seven died, three are still critical, 10 have minor breaks and concussions. They also lost two Astro Devils. What the hell happened?"

"I misjudged." John sighed. It was unmistakably laden with remorse. "I flew the *Grace* in subspace." John took a breath. "Ah, I flew it inside a star's gravity well. We were trying to lose three alien spaceships on our tail. Well, I got Jen to beef up the inertia-bubble to counteract the star's gravity so we could fly closer. I mean *really* close. We then jumped out, leaving the ships trying to shoot at us with a little present." Jason's confused look on his face spurred John. "I gave them a gravity wave. Well, I thought I had. I didn't realize that part of the wave was transported with us as we jumped to RHS."

Jason just stood there, dumbfounded. It was a brilliant tactic, except they materialized too near the space station and the *Versailles*.

"The gravity wave followed us to Rams Head and struck the *Versailles* and the station."

Jason shook his head in dismay.

"That's when the *Versailles* jumped to the EJP."

John bit his lip shaking his head. "Well, you saw the battering that the wave did to the *Versailles*; the station only had minimal shields." Jason's face dropped. "The wave hit the communications modules crushing half of the scientists inside. Most of the station crew were working in that module."

Once again, Jason just looked at John, his mouth open in disbelief.

"The station made it through relatively unscathed except for the comm module. We lost five good people ..." John had trouble finishing the sentence that confirmed the loss of those unfortunate scientists and engineers.

"It was bad luck they were all in the comm module," Jason tried to console. John said nothing.

"How did the Marines get killed? Did you leave them on the station before you left?"

"Well no, while we were searching for any survivors on the station, the Astrodevil patrol reported two contacts. The ships that were chasing us somehow followed us."

Jason's mouth just hung loose, his hands rubbing his temples.

"The two Astrodevils are still at Ram's Head?" Then the real implication of what John was saying struck Jason like a sledgehammer. "The two warships followed you... You fought them?"

"No, well, not exactly. There was only a third of one ship, and the other was pretty battered."

"But then that means ..."

"Yes, the third one got away." John watched Jason nod. "One of the ships had been cut in half, well to be more accurate a third, where only the first third arrived in Rams Head." John could see Jason hold his breath. "The second ship came through battered, but functional. I made the decision to board the vessel with *Aneska's* Marines."

It was at that point that Jason had to sit down. He shook his head, amazed at John's audacity. It was a gutsy move, considering. John could see Jason trying to figure if the Marines assigned to the merchant ships had boarding training. One couldn't be sure after the Battle for Earth. A lot of the original boarding parties were reassigned.

"...And that's how you've lost the two marines?"

"Yes. They hacked the midship airlock, Captain Waters, took two teams onboard, one towards the bridge and the other towards engineering. The men fought like demons against, nearest we can tell, thirteen different species."

Jason was shocked, "All on one ship?"

"Yes."

Jason shook his head.

John continued. "We need to recognize their efforts."

Jason nodded but held his tongue waiting for John to go on.

"Well the ship has been secured, and we have twenty-four aliens. I've got them locked in the brig and med bay of the alien ship for now. I've come back because I need some ships to patrol near RHS and some scientists for the captured warship."

It was Jason's turn to sigh heavily. *And it starts again... at least thirteen different species! What has he got us into?*

"Did you end up returning to the star?"

"No. I'll not go back until I have a few more ships. The aliens are likely on the lookout patrolling that area."

Jason let go of the breath he hadn't known he was holding. John could be impetuous sometimes.

"I was thinking of sending the ship to Cresseda," John said.

Jason looked confused.

"The ship and crew."

Jason's demeanor changed in the blink of an eye, he turned his head taking that far-away look. "Really? That's going to cause a stink."

John merely nodded. "I'd like to hold off telling the security council of this new threat."

Jason crinkled his forehead.

"Yes, I know that's exactly what they entrusted my mission with. However, I don't think that they are ready for the answer nor another enemy." John snorted. "They're still having difficulties getting their heads around dealing with the Lizards, let alone these new ones and the freighter."

"You haven't told them about the freighter with the Voyager disc on it?"

Jason stared at John. *He couldn't believe he hadn't told the Security Council about the freighter, Shit!*

A probe hand found an alien freighter that had crash-landed on a moon in what they dubbed the Color System. There were twelve planets in that system, each with an atmosphere with a different primary color. The freighter had been half eaten by something. But the worst of it was what they found in the cargo hold. The Voyager disc sent to space to invite aliens to Earth. Aside from the invite, the voyager hadn't had time to get far into deep space. *Some species took the disc from just outside our solar system. On our doorstep, in astronomical terms. They knew where Earth was...*

Jason ground his teeth. *Was John right to withhold the information from the Security Council?*

John could see Jason's mind working through the dilemma that John had just thrown into his face. "It won't be for long, just till we build a few more ships," John said as if reading his mind.

"So, you think Cresseda will get the best use out of it... the prize ships?"

Cresseda was one of the new human colony planets in the Harmony system. There were now five Human colony planets scattered in five systems. Each colony had grown to a population of ten to twenty thousand. Abigail had been teleporting heavy construction machines there for roads, clearing, anything. She had also included vats for the A-Bitumen used in construction. Most importantly she had included the specs for a new shipyard.

"Yes. Look, I'm on my way to Earth. I'll see you soon face to face. I've got a few calls to make. I'll pop in to see Josephine and her crew before I return to RHS. Take care of them while I'm gone."

Jason was a little surprised John knew the Captain's first name. Then again, John had changed in the last few years, just as he had.

John cut the comms before calling Abigail for an update of Cresseda's manufacturing capabilities. John explained that he needed a base away from Sol and Tau Ceti, not that there was a base there anymore after the *Godzilla* exploded. In that explosion, T.N. had suffered a major loss in scientific resources. Rebuilding there would take time and mental resolve. There was some debate that they should leave it for Earth Forces given its proximity to Earth. John wouldn't entertain a bar of that. Whether it was from guilt or its neighboring location, in his mind, it was precisely this reasoning as to why T.N. should still be there.

They needed to analyze and reverse engineer the new alien warship acquisition. Abigail had much the same reaction as Jason when he explained how he'd acquired it.

"They've barely started manufacturing the electric rocket engines." She said. "I don't think they are ready to take the ship and reverse engineer it. We have enough room for twenty or so scientists, but that will set back the manufacturing sector. We have a shortage of certified housing modules. Most of them are scheduled to go to Mardeen VII because they're still in the surface deployment phase. There are no domes, so they need it for the radiation and wildlife protection." This phase was when they set up the first planetside base after scanning and analyzing the planet's resource distribution. Each colony started with a space station above the planet that was their orbital warehouse, interstellar gateway, and a cargo terminal. But most importantly, it was a part of a satellite network surrounding the planet for uncovering resources and natural features of their new home.

John winced. It was not what he wanted to hear. Better to leave it to her to manage. However, they still needed to scale up their manufacturing capabilities. "What can I do to expedite Cresseda's capabilities?"

"Mechanical and civil engineers, 3d printers, robotics and a jump capable resource collection ship to mine the in-system asteroids."

"What?" John asked.

"Asteroid mining is becoming easier than mining the surface of a planet. We have a space crusher and solar smelter in place now, so we need a quicker way to find and retrieve the raw materials."

"Ok... I'll contact Ryan and Thurston to send you what they can." John moved to a serious tone. "Abigail, pulling the alien ship apart to see how it works is a top priority. I'll also be sending some military assets to keep it secure. We'll be upgrading the security with a full Garrison there on Cresseda because of all the new species that'll live there." John could see in her eyes the demands he was putting on her shoulders, like an oxen's yoke. He felt for her, she already looked tired.

"What else do you need?"

Abigail took a deep breath, then started to list out her problems and the solutions. The plan to start five Human colonies at once to mitigate the risk of Humanity being wiped out was a bold one, but it was facing lots of growing pains. It might all fall apart if they weren't careful.

John stayed longer than he expected at the main base in El Paso. He handed over his supply requirements to T.N. logistics. While on RHS, he had spent time downloading data updates of the stores and must-haves to repair the main systems. It also included the history of the situation from Rams Head and the *Grace*'s logs to the T.N. main servers. He loaded and encrypted extra pictures and video from the Marine armored boarding party marking them for command access only and sending a copy to Col. Eric Manders, the Marine arm of T.N.

John called Eric while the Colonel was inspecting the garrison at Dragon Trees spaceport. They needed marines to provide security for their new prisoners until they could be transported to one of the colonies in the Harmony system for internment. Cresseda had the Rice Space Station and also a small moon that could be used as a quarantine station. He guessed that eventually when the thirteen species arrived, the planet would specialize in xenobiology, and xenoanthropology (the study of alien cultures and how they developed).

Cresseda was a warm planet with breathable air, and a had a large mass of water. On the single largest continent that spanned from the north to south poles. The bulk of the landmass had a predominately cool climate that had a grassy steppe straddling mountains to the west and spectacular cliffs on the Eastern seaboard. Near the equator sat a volcanic island chain the locals called 'The Keys'.

Two hours later John spoke to Thurston for the loan of twenty scientists. They would start the investigation process on the warship then take their findings to Cresseda Aerospace Manufacture, a skunkworks based modular manufacturing division of T.N. Corporation. The Skunkworks took theoretical ideas and applied them to generate inventions or in this case, reverse engineered inventions. Out of that melting pot of prototypes, viable products would be produced that could be brought to market or used internally within T.N.'s war machine.

Caladan Underground Base Hospital, Titan

John's next stop was to the hospital on Titan to visit the crew of the *Versailles*. He made the rounds with the doctors to make sure they had everything they needed. Two of the crew had been transferred Earth-side for more extensive neurosurgery, the rest would be managed on Titan.

John walked into the small single room where Captain la Perouse lay staring at the wall sim of the Seine. The medical staff chatted quietly to each other in the corner over test results.

Nodding to the staff, he then approached the Captain's bedside. "Josephine, how are you feeling?"

The Captain tried to raise herself up from her pillows, so John gently laid a hand on her shoulder, and she sank back down.

"Admiral, I've felt better. I'm sorry we left before you got back to Rams Head. We were hit by something that came out of nowhere."

John felt giddy: she didn't know. "Er... Josephine, it was my fault. I returned from subspace too close to the station. We were being chased by three warships."

"You did this...?" Josephine stared at John, her small button nose angled just so, it made John squirm.

"Yes, I misjudged the effect the star's gravity would have through the jump." All the med staff, seeing this was a confession session, shuffled from the room uncomfortably. The Admiral had made a huge mistake returning to normal space so close.

"La Vache ... merde." (holy cow ... shit!) Josephine gave the Admiral a hard stare. "Votre vaisseau, *la Grace*?" (Your ship the Grace?)

"Yes." John felt the tension strain his whole body.

"You killed them, yes? L'extraterrestreals?"

"One dead ship, one captured and one escaped."

Josephine winced as she sat up straight in bed. Her ribs were bandaged, but she had still managed to put on pristine makeup. The tension dragged on awkwardly as she brushed a lock of her hair behind her left ear. A telltale that John recognized as she thought through a problem.

"Admiral, please give a warning *'before'* you need my help next time," she said with just a hint of a smile in the corners of her mouth.

"Captain, you have my sincere apologies, and yes, I will warn you." There was an audible intake of breath from the corridor.

"Admiral, I wish to see this warship when I get out."

"Captain, I am afraid you will see that, and more when you come back!" John stayed a while before he said his goodbyes.

When he arrived at the nurse's station, he asked to see the unit manager.

"Admiral? I'm Frances Higgins, the Hospital Administrator."

"Oh, I was expecting the Unit Manager."

"When a board member of T.N. comes to the hospital, they usually inform me a week or two in advance," she said perturbed.

"This was not official, Ms. Higgins. I came to check on the crew of the *Versailles*," John said, his relaxed manner disappearing.

"There is nothing wrong, then?"

"No, should there be?"

"Oh nooo... It's all fine, schtick and a-ok."

John frowned at Ms. Higgins. Looking around, he realized the nurse's station was enormous. "I didn't realize there was such a shortage of space for hospital bedrooms."

The Administrator seemed confused.

"Captain La Perouse's room."

"Oh, we put her in the broom cupboard, the smallest room in the hospital." Ms. Higgins smiled at her ingenuity.

"Why?" John said, with an edge to his question.

Ms. Higgins nodded her head as if it was obvious. "You know..." John was silent.

"Because her father accused you of stealing his invention. Some ray gun, thingy."

John had to bite his tongue. "Ms. Higgins, I appreciate your loyalty, but all the patients of this hospital will be treated with due respect. *Captain La Perouse has my full respect* and my thanks for risking her life for us all. Please ensure she gets the best room with the best care this facility can provide."

Ms. Higgins stood there, aghast.

John turned to leave. "Oh, and I would like you to ensure she gets flowers in her room. It's kind of dull in there for recuperating."

John made one final call to Squishy Isle. Tela and Drakmok identified the races crewing the alien frigate. The most important was the large cat that Captained the ship; it was called a Gnoll.

By the time John was ready to return to RHS, he had reconnected with Josephine and found she was in the best room of the hospital with flowers that adorned the walls and side table.

Chapter 27

Rams Head Space Station

When John landed the *Grace* on the hangar deck of Rams Head Station, he could see Jen was waiting for him with crossed arms by the control room; she didn't look happy. John could tell that she'd been grinding teeth as he could see her dimples and flushed cheeks. He couldn't help smiling inwardly and admire how beautiful she looked even when she was angry.

John waited till the last of his passengers had disembarked the *Grace,* saluting to Jen as they left the hangar deck making their way into the main station. He could tell the formalities of her rank still startled her; she could never get used to the constant protocol. It was one more thing to throw in John's face. He watched as Jen took a deep breath and walked to the base of the ramp directly in front of him and saluted. John was surprised by her use of the salute. She had never done that before, even in front of the whole battalion. Everyone knew that she never did, but that didn't matter. They all knew she was the genius who developed the antigravity projectors. John was still processing Jen's unusual behavior when he felt the sharp sting of the slap across his face.

"That's from me because you left me here in this godforsaken place away from Earth." John was taken aback trying to understand what she was talking about. He knew it was something he should know but asking Jen would invite another slap. He rubbed his tingling right cheek. Then it dawned on him: every time they were outside of the Sol system, they had been together on the *Grace*, until today!

"Jen, I thought you needed some time with your sister." John thought that was a weak reason, but nevertheless, it was one. The mere mention of Mags brought slow tears to her angry eyes. This time John dared fate by closing in and hugged her. Her tense body stiffened, then slowly as she released her anger, half-heartedly striking his chest with her fists, she fell into his arms.

She sobbed, dread seeping out. "She hates me, and I don't even know why. She won't talk to me long enough to tell me. She's too angry." Jen brushed tears from her cheek. "She must've suffered growing up, to be so spiteful and full of hate."

Jen's eyes moistened again. "I wasn't there to protect her." John wrapped his arms around her. She felt chill to his touch. She grabbed hold of him, drinking in his solid warmth around her. "I'm sorry, I've been so angry at you. I just don't understand why we didn't jump out when we had the chance, away from the star. You put me in an impossible position: I hate you and hate myself for it. I was so scared. I overloaded the gravity projectors so strongly that when we jumped here... I didn't think it would destroy the *Versailles* and kill all those people. They didn't need to die because of my stupidity!" Jen said, crying into his shoulder.

"Jen, the *Versailles* made it back to Ceres." Jen looked up into his eyes. "You shouldn't feel guilty, it's *me* that should take responsibility for it. It's as you say, we could have jumped earlier. It seems my caution about letting other species know of our jump capability, was overrated." John replied.

"What do you mean?"

"How do you think these Gnoll got here after us."

Jen blinked back her tears and took a moment to think.

"The ...?"

"Gnoll," John supplied. Quickly, he filled her in on what he had learned from Tela.

"If they have jump capability? They can get to Earth straightaway! What are we going to do?"

"I brought a lot more security, and some scientists to make a start on pulling apart their ship."

Jen started to bite her lip as she was prone to do when anxious.

John continued. "Although, some things don't add up. Why did only a third of the second ship arrive? The second big question is, where is the third ship?"

It just occurred to John, *if I was the aliens, wouldn't I send reinforcements here right now. He had left Jen here, unprotected!* John chastised himself again. "It just brings up more questions. My gut feeling is they don't have the tech, but I want to make absolutely sure of it."

Jen wiped her face and then gave John a reassuring smile. John could tell that she was still hurting badly, but he released his hold on her. He wished that he could take the whole responsibility for all those lives he just extinguished. But he knew her character, and that she was never going to let that happen.

John kissed Jen's wet cheeks and lips as they embraced. John felt the tenson between them ease just a little. Slowly he stepped back and smiled. "I have to check on security."

Jens shoulders slumped slightly. Regret flashed across his face as he turned and quickly contacted the station control center to keep alert for any contacts. He reluctantly made his way toward the control room: he wanted to check on the defense status of the station, especially since the *Versailles* was still in Sol system.

Jen stood there blushing as she watched John walk from the hangar deck. Despite his bullheadedness, he could be so gentle and loveable. "Damn him," she said to herself.

Chapter 28

Gnoll Home World

Lord Saga barely left her stateroom on their way to the Gnoll homeworld. The longer the trip took, the greater the dread she felt towards reporting her brother's death to their parents. Her father, Lord Valerian, would not take it well. Their misjudgment had cost them two ships, but more importantly, the leadership of the Pether family pride, and with it their hope for their family. Saga was under no illusions that her father favored her younger brother to take over the Family holdings once he had passed into maturity. Their mother had attached a gaudy golden hair clip onto Volund's mane, upon his latest registered victory, against a Bear-oBoar scout vessel. Volund had loved the clip. He clawed it every time she was around trying to make her jealous. Which infuriated her all the more.

Lord Saga's ship was directed by traffic control to the main launch pad attached to the south wing of the Pether

Sanctuary Compound. It was a short walk to the main hall from there. The soft leafy floor couldn't hide Saga's heavy dread-filled footsteps as she made her way through the reception chamber of her Family Pride. Large doors opened to admit her into the main hall where near forty Gnoll stood in formal attire chatting quietly. Banners tracing the Pride's four-hundred-year heritage lined the walls. Stark against the black stone, armor hung in pride of place behind the three high lord seating plinths. Toward the vestry on the opposite wall hung an ancient blood red cape with a faded Pether coat-of-arms. Down the armory wing stood mannequins wearing ancient metallic feline body armor with the family crest on their backs. Their vigilant scrutiny stood frozen in attack poses. Crossed claws painted with prominent blues and golds decorated the armor accessories. The rough-hewn material worn beneath the outer metal layer looked scratchy even if it could stop a glancing razor claw.

The silence of the courtesans betrayed their foreknowledge behind her visit. Word must have reached Pether that her brother had been slain. Pointed whispers crossed her hearing claiming shame and cowardice.

Padding up to the high lord plinths Saga knelt before her parents.

Her father bore his countenance regally as any King, edged in unyielding disapproval. Her mother matched his stern features with a resigned sadness.

Saga tipped her head then stood slumped before her parents not as their daughter but as a member of the Pether house.

"Lord Valerian, I bring grave news," she said in a meek tone barely looking up.

"Stand tall before me so we can see how far Pether House has fallen."

Saga straightened her back and dug her claws into the mossy floor. Slowly she looked up.

"Father..." Saga was cut short by the crippling snarl her father's stare wrought on her.

"Explain yourself," he commanded.

Saga described the small yacht and the chase. She spoke of evasive maneuvers and the shield within shields used by the little yellow container ship. When she got to the slingshot around the sun, Saga shed a single tear. She had yelled her voice hoarse on the journey home.

Whispers of weakness scattered throughout the hall amongst the Gnoll who could see her public display.

Her father stood on the mound, his claws digging into the synthetic dirt and grass floor. Anger contorted his face.

"Now is not the time for mourning. Compose yourself, cublet."

Saga felt the whip of his criticism. Calling her a juvenile was just too much, and she withered inside.

"This small ship" he continued, "that *you* were chasing, because your brother has no need for such an insignificant prize, destroyed two advanced Gnoll warships, and seriously damaged a third?"

"My Lord, the ship design was not within any authorized ship list." The 'ship list,' included all interstellar ship classes registered by the civilized species of the Galactic Collective. Any vessel class not on the list was deemed barbarian and therefore could be taken as a prize and kept without prejudice from any acknowledged species of the Collective.

"My lord, the ship ... could be a vanguard."

Lord Valerian just grunted. A vanguard vessel was a first contact ship. It was extremely valuable as it signaled a new race to be enslaved.

Valerian stared at Saga. "Why send such a small pathetic ship as a vanguard? I think not."

Saga was about to argue when her mother shook her head.

Lord Valerian continued, "Why are you alive and not your brother?"

"My Lord, Lord Volund was first among us who took the field of battle against the enemy. He was relentless in his pursuit of the vanguard ship," Saga replied, trying to remind her father of the value and not the size of the ship that mattered. Hopefully, her father believed her and not that her brother had taken a stupid risk on her behalf. Her father, given the opportunity, would lay the blame squarely at her feet.

"That is so. His character dictated he be first among many."

Saga winced at her father's reference that she was only one amongst many, not worthy of being a leader. *Did father not see that she was of his bloodline too.*

"Display the melee," he growled.

A large monochrome screen was brought into the hall, Saga's video ship's log showed ten feet tall. Snippets of her rowdy conversation with her brother echoed through the hall. Saga shrank in on herself.

"How is it that three warships were needed to chase down this little yacht?" asked Lord Valerian as he watched what records there were.

"The ship was indeed small but had very special abilities. It could maneuver in subspace like no other ship I have seen. It seemed to pass through the gravity well of the star that it was attempting to hide behind, *without* being destroyed." Murmurs from the courtesans were quickly quelled with a look from Lord Valerian.

"So, you're certain that the ship survived?" questioned the Lady of the House.

"No, my Lady, although the ship was not amongst the limited debris left within the system. It was a small ship which could have been destroyed or escaped. There was no debris from Lord Volund's ship either."

"They did not fly like they had a death wish, but they are alien." Saga shrugged. "The FTL drive signature was inefficient, it leaked plasma which would, on the surface, suggest a spacefaring race of limited capabilities."

"... or they just did not care to show their efficiencies," her mother interjected.

Saga watched her father as he considered her story and whether her judgment and the reports were accurate.

Lord Valerian frowned at his daughter; the story seemed unbelievable. *Turning on the point of a claw! Pfft. No race has done that, not even the Patron species have admitted to it.* He was disgusted at the recorded banter between the two siblings just before the battle. Lord Saga had acted childish and petty. He would not see such useless emotions cloud decisions, especially from those that would represent their house one day. He would send an investigator to verify the facts that she had presented.

"You escorted the remainder of the fleet to the trader station?" Valerian's eyes gazed down at her with an intensity born from many battles.

Lord Saga gulped. In haste, she had left the fleet to their own devices without protection.

Silence.

"You are lucky that another species wasn't near. Lord Tyron was conveniently at hand to escort the freighter convoy," her father said with a chill in his voice.

Lord Tyron... Noo, any Gnoll but him, she thought uselessly.

Saga realized that she had stuffed up. Why didn't she think to go back and escort the freighter convoy? It's what her brother would have done. *Stupid, stupid, stupid!*

"Your contract credits are forfeit and will be used to compensate Tyron's convenient assistance. You will return to the trader station and set straight our house accounts with the freighter Captains. You will then seek out this race of beings that threaten the Gnoll. Do not return until this species is known."

Saga was stunned by his judgment, her eardrums pounded. She barely heard the gasps from the court. She knew he would be harsh, but exile was unbelievable! That was something that she had never anticipated. She was his only blood and heir now. Steeling herself for the real conclusion, the harsh conclusion that she was not, in the Lord's mind, *of his blood*. She would never be the heir!

What about the return trip of the freighters to Gnoll homeworld? Who was going to escort them? Her father obviously didn't trust her anymore. It was just one more swipe of the claw her father meted out on her. There were few ships faster than hers in the Gnoll Kingdom. She may not get another escort run, but she would collect and settle the last one despite her father's swipe.

She thought furiously about her ship; it needed repairs, it needed to be upgraded. If this was the last chance that she would have of financial support from her family, she knew that she should get the ship upgraded as much as possible. This may be a one-way trip.

Saga stormed out of the hall and headed to the shipyards. She fumed while ordering as many upgrades as she dared on her ship. She focused on parts with longevity. Once the upgrade is complete, her first port of call, Antares Reach, to settle the accounts on the freighter escort run for her father.

The aggressive part of her mind cajoled herself into contacting her collective spy network to look for any ships with that little container bug like configuration or drive signature. She knew the pain of loss and shame would indelibly mark her. She will find this race of interlopers that had destroyed everything: her brother, her standing, her pride... she will unleash her wrath on the alien dogs that had killed her brother!!

Chapter 29

Brig, Rams Head Station

Captain Waters was having a difficult time. The Gnoll crew that had been captured were rebellious. Their actions border on the insane. Initially, the crew was relatively placid, however, as the time spent in captivity passed by, internal fighting amongst the dozen species was becoming lethal. Even the Human Marines were becoming reluctant to interfere in what seemed like inter-species politics.

Captain Waters urgently requested sociological assistance to determine what had made the prisoners so aggressive and restless.

"Captain, I believe the prisoners all think they will be executed," the sociologist said as she came to give Waters her report.

"What! Executed? We didn't say anything of the sort to the prisoners. We abide by the UN Universal Entity Law." The new law stated that all intelligent species were accorded equivalent Human rights.

"No, it's not the Humane treatment of prisoners. Apparently, in the big wide galaxy, many prisoners are executed, or alternatively, they are sent to some god-awful mine to be worked to death as slave labor."

The Captain shook his head. "Come with me, we are going to straighten it out."

The two headed into the mess area as the Captain ordered the marines to escort all the prisoners to attend.

The two Humans then looked at the group. The Gnoll Lord had been separated from his crew.

Capt. Ray Waters stood before the 26 crew and asked, "Who is the lead prisoner?" No one moved a muscle, head or claw. Ray knew that the prisoners would normally defer to the Gnoll Captain. However, when they separated him from his crew, the Servant species began to regain some sense of individual identity.

Finally, the sociologist pointed to one of the prisoners. "That old Ferret is one I had some success talking with, his name is Dymlock. He speaks Lizard tongue," she replied.

Waters signaled his sergeant to bring the Ferret forward. He then signaled his comms specialist to broadcast their conversation with the Ferret through the comm network so that all could hear.

"Translate what I say into the TRADE language," he said as his armband translator spoke in lizard tongue. The Ferret Dymlock shuffled forward and stood still for an agonizing minute. *"I would like to make this clear. When Humans make war or take prisoners, we follow rules and conventions. Those rules mean that you will not be executed. You will not be turned into slaves to be sent to the mines. You will be treated reasonably, assuming you cooperate.*

Cooperate... What I mean by co-operating includes no infighting, you assist one another, you follow directives from Human soldiers and those we assign as a leader. Dymlock, we now assign as a leader."

There were rustling murmurs throughout the group. Silence.

The Captain then turned on his heel towards the door. A pin could have been heard striking the deck given the reaction he received amongst the aliens. Waters ignored their stunned faces as he said over his left shoulder to Sergeant Timms.

"Sergeant, please have Dymlock escorted to my office, I want a little chat with the Ferret."

"Yes, Sir!"

◆◆◆

Brig Office, Rams Head Station

"I understand that you are what could be considered a representative of your crewmates?"

Dymlock just stood there, twitching his nose and grey whiskers curiously. "I am now, no thanks to you. They will all bring me problems."

"Well, that makes two of us."

The Ferret snorted.

"I hope you can reinforce what I said to your crewmates," Captain Waters reiterated.

The Ferret stood there for a long time then finally nodded his assent. He scratched a tangled knot of fur on his belly.

"How did you get on the ship?"

Dymlock frowned. "I walked."

"No, um..., why did you go on the Gnoll warship?" Waters asked.

Dymlock kinked his neck, his head tilted sideways curious at the question. "Like all others. Marines say with a gun, you do. Gnoll says with a gun... you do."

Waters didn't think the enormous Gnoll needed a gun for that, he had his paws, but he understood the principle.

"Do you wish to be on the ship?"

The Ferret laughed. "Is that a trick question?"

Water's face went red, he straightened his tunic. "The prisoners will be moved to a Human colony in Harmony system. The rest of the wounded will be transferred through to this facility once their wounds have been dealt with. Are there any special needs at this point?"

"No, Master."

"Don't call me that. I'm not, and I would never want to be a slave master."

Dymlock just shrugged his shoulders. He wasn't born in the last litter. Lower-level prisoners like ship's crew never survived very long after being captured. Most of them expected to be executed out of hand. Keeping prisoners was resource intensive.

Captain Waters sighed as Dymlock left his office.

♦♦♦

Gnoll Frigate *Light Bringer*, Rams Head Station

John led Jen through the hatch of the Gnoll hangar entrance. They had landed the *Grace* in the main bay of their prize warship.

"I wanted you to see this," John said as he halted before two huge drums with a large odd-shaped torus behind it.

John had brought her aboard to remind her of the positives to their misadventure, which had ultimately led them into the fight with the Gnoll. Jen had been isolating herself since her confrontation with Mags. The two were so similar and yet they were such polar opposites.

Jen looked at the fusion reactor without the normal intense curiosity he had seen fire her character. "The Germans had a similar design."

"Yes, the stellarator."

A muffled scrap came from the nearby back room. John and Jen looked at each other.

"It's supposed to be clear, the prisoners should be in the brig," John whispered.

Suddenly a Ferret with blue head fur and a red scar down one eye to his jawline rushed out from behind the drum to snare Jen's neck as she faced the opposite direction.

Jen cried out in surprise; the Ferret was fast and all claws.

The creature had a malicious grin on his face.

"Siisss hell cap now bad Creeep," he hissed.

Jen froze as the Ferret waved a wrench in the air near her face.

John raised his hands, then slowly reached for his pocket translator and switched it on. A small light appeared on the side. He hoped the TRADE that had been added was enough to give him an accurate translation.

"... give me what I want," the Ferret hissed.

"How about I give you your life while you tell us about the Gnoll." John pretended to scratch his cheek but activated his comm instead.

The Ferret tightened his grip on Jen's neck, his claws digging in drawing blood. The pain caused Jen to squirm.

"You been hiding all this time? You must be hungry," John said.

The Ferret unconsciously licked his lips.

"What's your name?" John continued.

"Glom. You killed other crew?"

"No, they're going to Cresseda."

"Not heard of it, I want to go Sirah."

"Sirah?" John asked.

"Trader Space Station."

"OK, we'll take you, but now you let her go."

"No, we sell this one and make a profit." Glom had a greasy smile.

John stared at Jen a moment before commenting. "This one is too skinny, plus its eyes are red and swollen; it must be infected."

Glom turned to examine Jen's face. John eased his pistol from his back holster and brought it round on the kidnapper. In one smooth motion, he pulled the trigger.

Jen's eyes bulged as the Ferret turned back and was pushing her into Johns line of shot.

The bullet whipped past Jen and grazed the ferret's head. Blood dribbled down over his scar. Glom glared and tightened his grip on Jen. "That will cost you."

Jen gasped as Glom squeezed harder.

Shit! I missed.

John held tightly onto his pistol, aimed at Glom's head. His second hand moved to support his grip.

"Your species is too weak and stupid. I watched you heal crew *before* Lord Volund. That was a mistake. Haha, he will kill you all for it." Glom's smile radiated evil.

John looked to Jen's scared eyes. Her trembling hands were desperately trying to get a handhold on the furry paw that held her neck. Her fingers slipped in the blood and fur as she tried to breathe.

Fighting down the terror at seeing her like this, part of John's mind registered the slippery ferret's words. So the Gnoll was called 'Lord Volund' was he? He filed it away for later. Mind racing, he tried another tack.

"You think us weak? That's funny since your warships are lying in pieces."

"The Gnoll are the pet dogs of the Sil'thik. All know this, except stupid humans. When the Sil'thik find out..."

"And you know because-?"

"Because I trade with the Sil'thik. They have nothing but contempt for the Gnoll. The furball shutzs!" Glom curled his scarred top lip showing his bloody yellow teeth. "Their noble families fight each other like starved lizards fight for food. Too many species that are better than you humans have failed to break into the Galactic Collective." Glom laughed.

"Why? Why did they fail?" John asked.

"Haha. If I knew I'd charge you the price of a moon."

"Well then you're no use to me, maybe I should just kill you now," John said, granite in his voice.

Glom adjusted his grip hand. John could see Jen's skin had turned purple and bloody from the clawed pressure.

"Why should I believe you trade with the Sil'thik. You're a lowly servant to Lord Volund."

A sour look overcame the Ferret. "How do you think he *became* Lord Volund."

John didn't trust those beady little eyes.

Glom took a deep breath. "My uncle Wulstan is a trader in Sirah. He contacted them, but I can introduce you to him."

"Why do I want to talk to this Wulstan?"

"He sells armaments made by the Insectoids," Glom said as if trying to justify the contact with his uncle was worth his life.

This was another reason that humanity had to be careful as they transitioned into the galaxy. Criminals must thrive in the Collective.

"Make me master of the ship, and I'll teach you how to live out here." He said, waving his wrench around.

"Haha. That's a generous offer." John rubbed his chin as if considering it.

Behind Glom, John spotted Mags holding an electro-rifle. He couldn't be certain, but when she shot the Ferret in the back with two electro bullets, she had a smile on her face.

Glom tensed as electricity sliced through his system. Arcs of blue ions jumped from Glom's wrench to the metal hairpin Jen wore.

Jen's expression froze as she caught the full force of the shock. She was touching Glom.

Both Jen and her kidnapper crumpled to the floor, their tangled bodies spasmed, releasing their body fluids, both rigid as they convulsed with excess electrical energy. When the two passed out from the shock, Mags walked out from her cover.

"Mmm, I guess I only needed one electro-bullet."

John looked back at Mags. He had the distinct feeling she already knew that. He wouldn't like to be in Mags' shoes when Jen woke.

Chapter 30

Squishy Isle.

Tela walked with an undulating swaggered toward the small yellow ship that sat on the edge of Squishy Isle Landing pad. Her mantel fluctuated between green::Curious:: and brown::Fear:: despite the reassurances given by her constant guard, Sgt. Marie Marcconi. Whenever Tela left the Isle, she was escorted, as much for her own protection as for her alien diplomatic status.

"Welcome aboard Tela," Jen said as she lightly grasped her fore-tentacle.

"I was surprised you requested my advice off-world. Are you sending me home?"

John looked at Sgt Marcconi, who shrugged her shoulders. "I explained to her that it was a consult only, and she would be back in her pool on the Isle when you're done."

Jen spoke up. "Please don't worry. You will always have a place here on Earth."

John turned from Tela back to Jen, his face muscles taut.

Tela's mid-tentacles fidgeted with shades of green::curious::. "Thank you."

Jen leaned forward, "I asked you here because we are doing a quick recon of the star system that we encountered the Gnoll ships."

Tela gazed back at John. "You seek their homeworlds?" she said as a statement.

"Yes." John looked uncomfortable.

Tela's mantle near her eyes discolored to black::distrust/deceit:: there was more the human was not saying.

"I asked you to come," Jen spoke up. "John did not wish to invite you because he thinks you are a huge security risk."

Tela looked back and forth between the Humans, Green::curious/uncertainty::.

Jen continued as John stared at Tela closely for any signs of malevolent intent.

"We have technology on our ship we do not want known to any, including other Humans."

"I see. I can keep quiet as the sands," Topaz::relief::.

John made a small nod, then turned to Sgt. Marcconi who straightened up and saluted at the unsaid order. Marcconi would make sure Tela didn't talk.

Tela watched the byplay as her mantle turned blue::sad::.

"Sgt," John said, "Please settle Tela in the passenger accommodation while we depart."

Just as Tela and Sgt. Marcconi were walking up the ramp, Tela turned and looked back at the spaceport terminal her tentacles tinged with orange::anger::. They weren't giving her time to get some necessities for a long trip. She estimated at least three months in a cramped small ship like this would be disastrous. These humans are more resilient than she thought.

"Sgt. Marie, I need Squishy things for the trip."

Marcconi tapped her earpiece to contact the Admiral and explain Tela's request.

Tela could hear John reluctantly give permission, but they needed to be back within the hour. No excuses.

"Thank you, Sgt. Marie," said Tela as she followed her out of the *Grace* and ran back to the Isle Spaceport Terminal.

John looked at Jen. Her neck had a bandage with a little blood seeping through. The cut from Glom's claw wasn't deep enough to need stitches. However, an inch to the right, and she would have been in serious trouble.

John had apologized profusely when she awoke from the effects of the electro-bullet, but the fallout from him shooting and missing the shot lingered. Despite his good intentions, he couldn't deny that it had placed her in more danger ... again. It was especially true when he backed Mags' use of the electro-charged tipped bullet. It was a good choice of weapon. Jen didn't seem to know that Mags' had shot twice and that the second charged rubber bullet was unnecessary.

So, feeling guilty, John was persuaded by Jen to allow Tela onboard for their recon of HP99012 where they met the Gnoll convoy. *'Having her there would curtail his reckless actions,'* she'd said.

Fifty-five minutes later the *Grace* shot through the atmosphere heading for Rams Head Station. John had been carefully making sure Jen and Mags did not meet. He had whisked Jen off to Titan Hospital to get her looked at. He told Mags to interview Glom and find out about the Gnoll and this Wulstan Ferret.

◆ ◆ ◆

"So, we're not waiting for more ships?" Tela asked. She stood at the back of the bridge. "You are hunting the Gnoll, yes?"

John nodded. "You said they are a servant species of high standing."

"Yes, I did." Tela's mantel drained to a dark brown::Fear::. Her mid-tentacles fidgeted, making odd shapes as she swayed.

John's neck flushed. He hoped they couldn't tell he felt guilty because he had promised to Jason that he would wait till they had several more ships available to escort them. Not just the one that hadn't had time for the paint to dry. The *T.N. Macau* that came directly from the dockyard and was barely operational. It had no FTL capability only sub-light engines. The *Grace* would need to transport it first before it jumped itself.

"It's a fine ship." The fast attack ship was a frigate.

"It's not even finished!" Jen shook her head. "John, it hasn't had its shakedown cruise."

"Look, it doesn't need to move much. It's got guns and shields. We've tested them."

Jen shook her head and looked to the ceiling.

Tela turned to Sgt. Marcconi and whispered, "Are they mating?"

Marcconi stifled a splutter. "Not exactly."

"They should and quickly before they kill us."

"Yes, you're probably right."

◆◆◆

HP99012, Waypoint 3 to Sirius

Jen teleported the *T.N. Macau* to the outskirts of HP990012 half an hour before the *Grace* joined the frigate. Getting through the first two waypoints had been slow, but the third had been completed quickly and efficiently.

"I'm picking up the *Macau* and a small stealth probe. There are no bogies," Max said from his com console.

John let out a breath. They planned to drop a few stealth probes to help track the Gnoll if they reappeared.

"Set a heading for the ringed planet. We'll place another probe there. Max, contact the *Macau* to drop another probe in the asteroid belt."

The two ships fired up their electric engines and headed in-system.

Four hours later when the *Macau* was deploying the second probe they were interrupted. A ship appeared on passive scans of the system outskirts. Their captain gave orders to shut down and receive passive scans only. A tight tachyon beam comm signal was sent to the *Grace* warning them of the new arrival.

Bridge, Gnoll Frigate *Rip from Above*

Lord Tyron watched the scans for alien ships. "Are you certain this is the right system?"

"Yes, my lord. I retrieved the location from the freighter logs myself."

Tyron smiled. Lord Saga was as ambitious as she was reckless. Leaving her freighter convoy was foolish. He laughed at the news that she had been exiled by her father no less. The Pether pride was going down; their iron influence over the King had finally been broken. They just didn't know it yet.

Tyron looked at the galactic clock. It was based on the pulsing of several stars and triangulated to the Tri-Galfrey system. Using only one star created problems when one considered that space stretched, warped and folded.

"They're late."

Nobody contradicted the Gnoll lord.

Bridge, *T.N. Grace*, Ice Rings of HP99012-c

"Max, what are they doing?" Max was scanning the Gnoll frigate with *Grace's* tachyon sensors.

"It's hard to tell, but I think it's just stopped."

Jen looked over to the Squishy who was transfixed by the holo representation of the star system. It was weird that Tela had never seen such a display. Jen recalled on the pirate ship, the *Kato*, they had screens with green monochrome pictures. They weren't even in color like on a basic vid screen or TV. It was obvious to Jen that it only just occurred to Tela that the Humans had *much* better technology than in the civilian trade center built for the Squishys.

"Is this normal Tela?" Jen asked.

Tela blinked and focused on Jen. "Ahh, no. I don't think so. Looks like they are waiting for someone."

Two hours later ...

"Still nothing."

"Nothing." John sat back in his chair. The Gnoll lord they had captive at Rams Head Station was not patient. John worried that Lord Volund was atypical for a Gnoll and so their plans would need to be revised.

"Contact, whoa! It's big."

"Is that a Gnoll ship?" John sat wide-eyed.

"No. That's a Bear O-Boar Catlin Class ship." Tela started to shake, her mantle turning a deep freckled brown::Fear::, like the ocean floor.

"A what?"

Tela ignored the question, her breathing catching in short quick breaths as a pungent sea salt smell permeated the bridge. "Why would they meet the Bear O-Boar, their enemies, when the Sil'thik are their patron."

Jen looked back at the main viewer where it displayed a zoomed-in sim generated picture of the alien ship. She remembered Tela's homeworld had been destroyed by the Bear O-Boar.

"The Gnoll frigate is moving to intercept."

♦♦♦

Meeting the Bear O-Boar

The two alien ships nestled to each other like bosom buddies. Their meeting had continued for what seemed like hours, but in fact, it was less than one.

"Well that was short and sweet," John said, trying to make light of the situation for Tela's sake.

Once the larger Bear ship disengaged, it sped off outward bound from the gravity well. After an hour, it had disappeared off their scopes.

♦♦♦

Bridge, Gnoll Frigate, *Rip from Above*

Lord Tyron laughed out loud. The Bear O-Boar had paid handsomely for the intel on a new species with remarkable ship handling. This new relationship with his Patron's enemy was finally paying off. Several more of those payments and he would be able to buy a small planet. His Pride had been outcasts for so long that their *claws had grown into the dirt*. This was an expression used to denote powerless; stuck in the dirt unable to hunt like real Gnoll. Of course, they would have to pretend to invade the planet to satisfy the Galactic Collective's legal annexation requirements. However, once Tyron transferred the credits, it would be handed over.

"A ship has just entered the system."

Lord Tyron snarled at the sensor operator. "Who?"

"Ahh, Lord Saga."

Tyron's eyes narrowed. Had she seen the Bear O-Boar ship?

"The *Wild Roar* is on an intercept course. Time to intercept three hours."

"Incoming message from Lord Saga."

"Tyron, what are you doing here?" Saga's voice was harsh and graveled.

"Just visiting the site of your downfall." The words had a joyous tone that stung.

"Tyron, Nigire Pride is nothing, will be nothing but a laughing stock for farmers like yourself." Saga was only too happy to continue the blood feud between the two Prides.

"See that your words don't bite your tail, Saga. The Nigire Pride is in ascension and will leave you starving and clawless. Tend to your own house, cublet." Tyron disconnected the comm.

Bridge, *T.N. Grace*

"We've got a general direction of where the two Gnoll ships came from," John said optimistically.

"Pfff," was all Jen could say. "That direction expands out in a cone exponentially."

"Ummm, guys. I don't know if you've realized, but that Gnoll ship will run right near the *Macau*. There's no chance she'll remain undetected."

"Damn. You're right."

"We can't leave her there."

"If we do teleport her out, we'll light up like a Christmas tree." John looked over at Jen, who was already biting her lip.

"Ok Jen, line her up."

There was a sudden flash in the asteroid belt. Shortly after, the two Gnoll warships turned and headed directly for the *Grace* just as predicted ...

Chapter 31

Bridge, *T.N. Grace*

John, Jen, Max, and Tela stood around the tactical plot table near the rear of the bridge. A holographic of the solar system turned slowly displaying the movements and trajectory of each ship and the celestial bodies.

The *Grace* had maneuvered into the outer rings of the gas planet, HP99012-c. The light from the sun erupted in a brilliant shower of blue and white crystalline refraction.

"What are the rings made of?" asked Tela. Her voice was suddenly strained.

Jen gasped at the beauty cast from the rocks between the *Grace* and HP99012's sun. The crystalline form of the rocks refracted the sun's rays in a magnificent light show like the one you'd see in the early hours of New Year's Day. The main viewer had zoomed close to the rings highlighting the blues and whites within the rocks.

Max pulled up the geo-survey that was done by the probes.

"Um, some frozen nitrogen, oxygen, hydrogen, heavy metals but mostly methane ice."

Tela gasped. "Turn the engines off now!"

Everyone looked at the Squishy.

John was first to react striking the engine kill switch. It was usually only set when they were planetside and when people could be near the engine mounts.

Tela shuffled, "Methane ice is highly flammable – the *boom, boom* kind. If the engine exhaust touches one of the rocks and heats it too much, it may detonate."

"But there's no atmosphere to transmit the explosion," Jen said.

"The fragmented rocks would hit the ship," Tela countered.

Jen nodded in understanding. Diamond hard shards would probably pass right through their shields. Especially the weak point near the engines where it's heated.

"What, you're telling us we're in a natural minefield?" asked John.

Tela makes a crooked smile and raises her fore-tentacles in an expanding action, "boom, boom."

"I wish she'd stop saying that," complained Max.

All eyes diverted to the hologram with the oncoming Gnoll warships.

Slowly the *Grace* moved forward, careful not to throttle the engines. It quickly became apparent that the Gnoll will be able to fire on them before they would not get through the ice field.

"Jen, can you make the gravity projector shaped like a cone we can put at the front of the ship?"

Jen stared at John.

"Are you serious? I'm not a magician." John and Max just stared at her, believing she could do anything with the grav projectors.

Slowly she shook her head, looking at the ships inbound. "No. Not before they get here." She nodded her head at the holo.

"What about a strong gravity bubble away from the ship, to drag the rocks there?" John said.

"No," she said, shaking her head again. "Rocks are light compared to the ship, it will drag them from *both sides, through* the ship."

Max cut in. "The ships are closing fast, thirty minutes before they are in range."

"There must be something we can do...?" John stared at Jen.

"Quiet! I'm thinking." Jen's eyes flared.

"Time to jump ready?" John queried. His whole concentration centered on steering the *Grace* behind the gas giant out of direct laser line of sight of the Gnoll.

"Thirty-five minutes," Max replied.

The two Gnoll ships were zeroing in on the *Grace* from the far side of the system past the sun. The little yellow ship hung, stuck in the ice belt, trying to fly behind the gas giant.

◆◆◆

Bridge Gnoll Frigate, *Wild Roar*

Saga screamed at the screen, "Tyron you grass eater, they're mine!"

Tyron's ship, *Rip from Above,* had beaten Saga's vessel by ten minutes. They were both ecstatic when the small yellow ship seemed to suffer some engine trouble. It was only working at a tenth of its known speed when it was chased by Saga and her brother in their first encounter.

Now, Tyron would breach their hull and claim '*kill rights*' of the vanguard ship and all it represented.

"Energy build-up in *Rip from Above,* they are preparing to use their main lasers."

Saga's eyes were fixed intently on the main viewscreen that showed the two ships. "Power lasers."

The Ferret crew rushed to obey lord Saga's command.

"Target *Rip from Above*."

The tactical officer stared at Saga in disbelief.

Saga turned to the Ferret, "Do it!"

Before she could turn back, a blast struck the front and side shields of *Ripped from Above* knocking them both out. Explosions rippled along the gunwale. Slowly the ship turned to expose their working shields toward the small yellow alien ship. It was certain, one more shot and Tyron would be done for.

Saga's head snapped back toward the tactical officer, a *'We didn't shoot, did we?'* expression on her face.

The Ferret quickly shook his head.

This was the first time that Saga considered that the little ship may be much more dangerous than she originally believed. Her single ship may not be enough to take down the yellow bug ship.

♦♦♦

Bridge, *T.N. Grace*

"Gnoll ship Alpha has an energy build-up. No, both now have energy charging."

John glanced at Jen to see if she had any brilliant ideas. Her fingers flew over the pullout keyboard. *My God,* he thought, *she was scripting something. Scripting takes forever let alone testing it... We got no hope.*

The first of the two Gnoll frigates slowed to enter the deadly planetary rings of rock. Their haphazard steering suggested they weren't aware of the dangers.

"Reassigning grav projector energy to shields," John said quietly.

Jen stopped mid-keypress. She turned to John with a raised left eyebrow.

Suddenly a series of explosions rocked the *Grace*. Low-level radiation warning alarms sounded in the background.

"The dumbass fired on an ice rock! Ha, it blew their shields," chuckled Max.

"What's a doomass?" said Tela.

"It's somebody like Kane," Sgt. Marcconi suggested.

"Ahh, yes a doomass," she said, flexing her pink Mantle skin skirt.

John returned his focus to steering the *Grace* through the rock field.

"Shards... we can't track them all," Max complained. "Bandit alpha has multiple explosions. Its shield is down!"

All looked at the holo display and the energy signature readings.

"The Bandit Alpha has turned aside. Their new heading ... 045 declination 11 degrees."

"How odd. That's where they came in. Surely they wouldn't have come directly from their home planet?"

John said with a smile. "It's worth checking out. We may find a Gnoll controlled world on that heading."

"Aaah, still trapped here," Jen said, exasperated.

"What's going on with the second ship?"

"It's just sitting there... like a shark of the deep is awaiting its prey to swim from the shallows so it can strike," Tela said. Her body convulsed in a shiver, her mantle spotted brown::fear:.

♦♦♦

Bridge, Gnoll Frigate, *Ripped from Above*

Slowly *Ripped from Above* left the system. The vessel's shields fluctuated highlighting the problems still onboard the ship from the devastating methane explosions.

Lord Tyron roared.

He had risked everything to get the Pether Pride internal council memos. Saga must have kept some information back otherwise why meet the small yellow ship aliens.

He knew the yellow ship had seen him meet the Bear o-Boar. How could they not? *Whoever they are, they had to die!*

Suddenly an environment alert sounded. Lord Tyron turned to his seat console. Three of the four warning lights flashed against a picture of the four vats that generated oxygen. "Environmental, report."

"We've got contamination in vats 1 to 3. We've isolated vat 4." The vats contained fast growing plumes of oxygen algae.

"Contamination, from what?"

"High trace readings of crystalline methane and lithium hydride. It's killed the production and the base culture.

We'll have to return to port to replenish it. With only one vat, it will turn toxic within the week from overuse. We have to clean and sterilize the first three vats before we can cultivate."

Lord Tyron gritted his teeth. All the universe is conspiring against him. His prize is right before him in that field of ice rock, now Saga will get it.

A cold light glimmered and suffused his eyes. *Unless he killed her before she returned to Gnoll space.*

"Helm, head for HiggramIII."

"Yes, my lord."

♦♦♦

Bridge, Gnoll Frigate, *Wild Roar*

"Ha. Serves the furball right," Lord Saga admonished as she watched Tyron's ship turn and head out of the system.

The little yellow bug ship was making slow but steady progress through the field of methane rocks. Analyzing their route, she wondered how she was to catch the bug ship. The trip from the shipyard hadn't lightened her mood. Her planned upgrades had been stalled, no doubt by her father. She needed enough to show progress. Especially now that Tyron had caught the scent of the bug ship. How he found out was a mystery, but she suspected

Lord Egress' distant relatives. She had never liked him or his family.

"Target their sub-light engines," Saga said. "half-rack EMP missiles." If it worked, it would take out the *Grace's* electronics leaving it vulnerable and adrift.

"Fire."

♦♦♦

Bridge, *T.N. Grace*

"Missiles inbound," Max squirmed in his seat.

"Point defense is still offline," came a voice through the comm from engineering.

"Gatlin guns!" John flipped the *Grace* so the larger machine guns could aim. "Linking point defense targeting to gatlins," she said. These guns, usually found on attack helicopters, spewed out thousands of rounds a minute.

The bullets left the gun on a ballistic course. It was a calculated risk. Normal point defense missiles homed in on the aggressor missile adjusting for radical changes in flight and attitude. Analysis of the lizard battle showed many of the Lizards missiles were ballistic, and those few that were not were guided by a lizard gunnery operator. They hoped that the Gnoll were just as bad as the Lizards at miniaturized electronics.

"Three missiles destroyed, it's working!"

Suddenly another explosion from the natural methane rock mines floating in the rings near the *Grace*.

"I think I have something," Jen said. "I'll create reflective donuts at the stern that increase in size toward the hull. It then acts *like* a cone to push the rocks aside."

Through the viewport, the command team could see electrical discharges ripple two feet above as they traveled along the second inner shield. Much like the Aurora Borealis, the hazy green and blue colors surrounded the ship.

Alarms and warning lights flashed on John's console as several EMP missiles detonated off the port side, frying the less hardened electronics.

The bridge was cast into darkness briefly before red emergency lighting took over.

"Sub-light engines, jump drive, gravity projectors, defensive weapons are offline. Life support, offensive weapons and shielding are active," said an androgynous voice.

"Loading the worm torpedo," Max said. The worm was an offshoot of the spy tech developed by the Chinese to spy on T.N. Corporation. Once it breached the hull of a ship, it burrowed in and sniffed out the nearest source of EM comms to dredge any information and transmit it back to the *Grace*. It was one of the few chemical rockets in their arsenal.

He had little hope the worm would work. They did load other decoys to launch at the same time. He saw it as a form of targeted active EMP. Even if they did work, they needed to be in range to receive any transmissions from the worm.

"Firing," he said. At least he did *something*, rather than announce pending doom.

John used the gatlin to target and weaken a small area of the *Wild Roar's* shield.

The torpedo's size was massive compared to a normal missile. It would scare any ship that saw it homing in on them. Assuming it had nukes inside.

The torpedo's small launcher charge fired, pushing it away from *Grace's* hull before it ignited its main chem thruster. The torpedo drove through space, dodging the broken rocks that littered the route to strike, seconds after the electrically charged bullets fired by the Gatlin gun as they hit the alien ship's shields.

The armor plating of the torpedo stripped from its frame as the alien ship's shield tried to block its path. The inner rubber pod passed through the shield to splat against the *Wild Roar's* hull.

An A-bitumen glue-like substance oozed out of the shell against the hull, sealing any leak around its perimeter before a drill bit made of diamond teeth cut into the hull. Twenty small spiderlike machines scurried in through the hole seeking EM hotspots to retransmit any signals it found back to the hull breach and then tachy signal to the *Grace*.

Spider 05 crawled along a narrow air duct towards the bow of the ship. Its EM sensor detected a large source up ahead.

♦♦♦

Bridge, Gnoll Frigate, *Wild Roar*

"What is that?! It's huge! Shoot it!" Saga pointed to the scanned signature of the torpedo fired from the *Grace*.

The micro-electronics in the brain of the torpedo set it twisting and turning with complex evasive maneuvers.

Saga's eyes widened as she waited for the nuclear detonation. The thing had got through their shields somehow.

Nothing.

Lord Saga sagged in her chair. Their weapon must have failed.

"What was it that they shot at us?" Lord Saga asked.

"Unknown my Lord. It moved like the wind. I have never seen such reflexes before." The tactical officer had assumed the torpedo had been manually controlled like all missiles on Gnoll ships and what he knew of the Collective. They had heard the lizards used self-guiding tech, but it probably meant some bio-hybrid. Even then, it was only a rumor.

"Whatever it was, it failed to explode. Given the size of that thing, it probably would have blown us up. How did it get past our shield?"

"Unknown."

"Pull us away from them. We don't want them to send another large missile that works."

The helm slid a T-shaped controller to the side as the thrusters pulled the *Wild Roar* away from the ring of floating ice rocks.

"The little ship seems to be picking up speed." The *Grace* headed further into the ice field. The rocks were pushed out of the way as if an invisible hand swept them aside.

"Shall we follow around the edge of the field, Lord Saga?"

"No." The crew were stunned at her response. "They are too powerful for us. We need more ships. Make a recording of this battle for my father."

Bridge, *T.N. Grace*

Jen sat back releasing a breath. Her workaround to create three donut-shaped gravity fields at the front of the *Grace* to push the rocks aside was working. At the bow sat the smallest with each larger field placed in sequence, so it made up a rough cone-shaped repulsion field. The *Grace* strained to move forward.

The field was of similar shape to what they used around the *Grace* to reduce drag when it flew within the atmosphere. The greatest concern was to prevent the rocks from striking each other and shattering into shards as they tumbled away through space.

Jen looked at John, flabbergasted that the aliens, they now knew to be Gnoll, weren't firing on them or chasing them down. It was unclear what had changed their minds.

The first ship had suffered only minor damage as far as they could tell but left all the same. Jen didn't like inconsistency. It made the aliens unpredictable.

Suddenly Max yelled, "Whoo Hoo!" Jen and John both turned to stare. "Those sneaky Chinese. The worm just got into a data stream. We are picking up fragments of ... something."

"Really, what?"

Max shrugged his shoulders. "It could be their record of toilet flushes for all I know. But we do have something," with a big grin.

Jen turned back to the small tactical hologram between her and John on the main console. "Look, they're leaving," Jen said her eyes wide. It was true, the ship had turned and was following the first Gnoll ship's heading. That can't be a coincidence, surely.

With a sneaking suspicion, she thought they may have just found a vector for a Gnoll world. Jen looked over her shoulder at Tela, who saw the same implication. They had found their bully species.

Chapter 32

Cresseda Colony, Harmony System

The *T.M.N. Aneska* took nearly a month using A-Drive tech to move the crew from the Gnoll warship, *Light Bringer* to a small Human colony called Cresseda. Two gunships escorted the *Aneska* when it transitioned from subspace to Rice Space Station orbiting the planet. Small cargo shuttles and mining barges of processed ingots filled one of the two docking arms.

The space station was the central solar and interstellar terminal for Harmony system where all ships docked. It acted as a customs and quarantine gateway station. Only Human ships with friendly transponders were permitted to land on the planet. Not that any non-friendlies had approached the planetary system. A ring of small sensor satellites had been placed in orbit to detect any offending ships.

Most cargo container pods transported from Sol to Harmony would either materialize at 9am every two days in space nearby with a transponder. Tugs could then find, net them and drag them into the space station collection hold for processing and distribution to the planet's surface. Precious cargo like people or new technology were sent by ship like the freighter *T.M.N. Aneska* for safety reasons.

Despite its shaky beginnings, Cresseda had a small but thriving manufacturing base which focused on shipbuilding. A small yard had been built where it produced cargo and gunboat class vessels. The ships were easily configurable using specialized replaceable modules for defense or merchant use. Although the gunboats could be linked to create a massive warship, they lacked the cohesive operation and structure of a purpose-built warship. John had plans to triple the size of the dockyard basing it in space to allow them to build frigate-sized or warships.

Among the newest alien-friendly buildings built in Sol and teleported to Cresseda, was an interspecies accommodation and research center. Each wing had upgraded environmental controls to suit different species' needs. Small arboretums were included. The beautiful furnishings came with built-in spy tech to learn all they could from their guests.

When the prisoners got to the research base, Captain Waters ground his teeth as his men complained at the luxurious accommodation given to the aliens. His crew were billeted with the marine garrison which was far more spartan than the prisoner's accommodations were.

"These are our homes?" Dymlock said in disbelief.

"Yes. We do not know your species, and we desire to learn all we can about you."

Dymlock was quick on the uptake. "So, we are lab rats?"

Captain Waters didn't answer at once. "For the moment." He knew the Ferret thought about when he would be dissected like a scientific specimen.

Waters cringed at his order to place them there. He would speak to his superiors, these people were as much victims as any, and shouldn't be treated like Ferrets in a cage.

'The Keys', Cresseda, Harmony System

The *Grace* materialized from subspace in Harmony System and headed for the 'The Keys' on Cresseda, the only Earth-like planet in the system. Two gunboats powered toward the *Grace* on an intercept course. John transmitted his clearance code where the Cresseda Spaceport Control (CSC) matched it to their records and his recorded transponder.

"*Grace,* this is Cresseda Spaceport Control, Welcome to 'The Keys' Admiral. Pad two-five-zero has been assigned to you. Set ILS to Alpha-Seven-Seven-Hotel. Is there anything else we can do for you, sir?" A copy of the conversation appeared as text on John's screen with links to further information. A semi-transparent corridor also appeared on the main viewer, to help John guide the *Grace* to the designated landing pad. John grunted with satisfaction at the upgraded security and traffic control measures.

"Please give Governor Willoughby my greetings and ask for a meeting at his convenience."

"Yes, sir."

John brought up the telescopic view of the peninsula and surrounding islands called 'The Keys'. As he came on final approach to the spaceport, he could see a clash of cultures. Many of the buildings had rounded roofs and arches with a natural red clay color to them like those he had seen on Traynor in the Lizard colony. Unlike the Lizards, Humans tended to stick to modern glazing materials such as carbon nanotubes, glass, and tiles.

The Keys was an experimental interspecies colony where Lizards, Humans and now the thirteen species that made up the Gnoll crew were building their homes together. It was very early days yet, but John had a good feeling about it.

He smiled to himself. He had a present for the Lizard leader Darvus. The front of the second Gnoll warship was sitting in his cargo hull.

"You're enjoying this, aren't you?" Jen asked.

"I think we are doing good things here."

"And adding the Gnoll crew here?"

"Gives it a more cosmopolitan flavor, don't you think?"

"Pfft," Jen blew out. A small smile brushed the corners of her mouth. John smiled despite the bandage still covered the marks left by the Ferret.

Jen studied the now lined face of her companion. John had aged over the last few years since she'd first met him. It was not surprising given the constant pressures he was under. She resolved to get them both a couple of days on the pristine sandy beaches here where, just maybe, they could talk about the Rams Head debacle and John's bad aim with a pistol. It wasn't called 'The Keys' for nothing.

John watched as another shuttle flew past *Grace*'s port side with large amounts of foods and essentials which were being imported into the colony, helping it start up. John could have sent the Gnoll alien technology to the other Earthly powers for research. However, he was feeling vindictive given how much grief they had caused T.N. recently as they scrambled for all the Lizard tech.

Lizard Compound in 'The Keys'

Darvus was proving to be an excellent leader, guiding not only the Lizard contingent but also the Human contingent, despite the ill feelings many Humans had towards the Lizard population. John and the Dept. Head of Interspecies Relations had been careful to pick Governor Willoughby, who was a strong but thoughtful negotiator. They needed somebody who could think creatively. Setting up a multicultural colony that included aliens was certainly that. The main compromise was a significant military presence that was officially independent of all sides of government. Adding the Gnoll crew would stir the melting pot, and hopefully not become a pressure cooker.

Chapter 33

UN Security Council, Geneva, Earth

Jen and John's quick visit to the beach in the Harmony system was only a small reprieve from the Earth side politics that were awaiting him on his return. John always got a bad taste in his mouth when he had to meet the UN Security Council. Yes, they had supported his information gathering. Frankly, they had no choice. On paper, it looked good for their respective governments.

"Will the information you are gathering with your probes be generally available to the International Community?" It was no surprise that the French representative had broached this question. Although the French had contributed to the war fleet that defeated the lizard's, their main interest lay in starting up new colonies. They wanted to mine T.N.'s data on nearby planets suitable for colonization.

"We will no doubt inform you of any pending invasion that we know about. Some data may be available under a purchase agreement. I would need to talk with our finance group as to its value," John said.

The Frenchman stood to complain, but the house chairman banged his gavel quietening the room.

"We see you're making progress building a gateway, for lack of a better word, at Rams Head. Is it your intention, to become a customs platform for the rest of the world?" said the American representative.

John was surprised at their information. "Yes. However, this gateway is only temporary until we have a better understanding of what species are out there and what their capabilities are. We have heard of a Ferret trader species, and we are keen to make contact with them. Before we do, I believe we need to build our war fleet for defensive purposes."

"Once again, we are confronted with T.N. taking the bulk of spoils from the trade deal with this new Ferret species while the rest of Earth Forces gets the crumbs," said the Australian representative.

"Need I remind the Council, that T.N. takes the bulk of the risk. If the Australians want to take the lead, we will step aside and endeavor to assist them with the same enthusiasm they have shown us."

"Umm, er, that won't be necessary."

Two more hours of badgering and John finally got out of the meeting. They gave him the approval to contact the Ferret run Finer Trader Station to start a trading dialogue.

John neglected to mention how they were going to contact the Ferrets and in what capacity; as a Patron or Servant. There was also no mention of the Gnoll. John wondered how long before that got out.

Oval Office, Washington

The President stared back at the General, who seemed nonplussed by the report he was giving. "General, your last attempt to take T.N. technology was a dismal failure. Not only did we not get the tech, but we also lost the *USSF Arlington*, our only interstellar spaceship. Thankfully we have built four more to replace it. Three are still hidden in Alaska. Now you propose to use them to capture the Rams Head Station?"

The General's left eyelid twitched uncontrollably from the President's scrutiny.

"Our new ships are a lot more capable now."

President Avery eyed the General then turned to his Science Advisor, Dr. Kelly Anderson. "What of the technical assistance T.N. has given with spaceship design?"

Kelly looked at the General then back to focus on the President. "We are making remarkable progress. Much of the knowledge gained was incorporated in building those ships the General is so proud of. I would hate to see it dry up over a disagreement, like high jacking Rams Head."

The President flinched at her straight, unlawful assessment.

"Having somebody infiltrate RHS to steal or redirect the alien tech would produce a much better result than an all-out attack."

President Avery nodded. "Get it done."

Kelly departed the office, leaving the General and the President alone.

The President looked around the room as if trying to spot any bugs. "What of this Gnoll species they are keeping at RHS?"

"All we know is that it's some sort of feline," said Gen. Abercrombie. "Vicious as hell."

"Do we know what their plans are yet?" "Not yet. However, I'm hopeful to see something from my operative on the station soon," the General boasted.

"So, for now, we play nice."

♦♦♦

Observation Lounge, Max's Station, Titan orbit

"So, do you think that Darvus and his team will work together with humans on the Gnoll tech?" asked Jen as she plonked herself in a chair near John. Elvis walked to the bar and grabbed three beers and some crisps before coming over to the observation windows. His five-day growth comically made his chin look hairier than the top of his skull. Elvis had recently returned from his mission to Canopus. He was here to personally report to John on what he discovered.

John broke his concentration and stared at Jen for a second. "I'm not certain, but with any luck, they'll trust us."

Jen frowned at his response. "You didn't give them the tech for reverse engineering?"

"Not exactly."

"You gave it to them to build up trust," Elvis added as he joined the conversation.

John nodded his head. "We have some good people, who would be able to reverse engineer it. At the very least we could have given it to Earth Forces. Although it's a risk giving it to Darvus, I think the benefits of his trust far outweigh the short-term gain the tech gives us."

Jen stared at John. "You're a shark," she said, smiling.

Before Elvis could voice his opinion, John was already staring out the window to the turmoil below.

"We now have our target bully," John said without turning.

"You mean the Gnoll?" Elvis said.

John turned, his eyes downcast.

"They attacked us first," Jen said frowning.

"If we follow Tela's advice to the letter, we'll be declaring war," John said dejectedly.

Elvis looked at John's dispirited figure. "I wouldn't say that's nothing, because sometimes bullies get what they deserve. *'Karma's a bitch'* as they say...." John didn't move. "Maybe it won't come to that."

"Yes, maybe it won't come to that," echoed Jen.

No one spoke for a minute, each was caught within their own thoughts.

Elvis turned to Jen, "Do we have a Plan B or even a Plan A regarding the Gnoll?"

"Aside from Tela telling us to pick a fight, the plan is kind of loose. Well, actually it's non-existent. I'm sure someone will come up with something."

Elvis nodded. "The way that stuff develops around here, I'm not surprised."

"Any news on the derelict freighter that was nuked?" John asked Elvis.

"We know the nuke came from Earth from its radioactive decay signature. Bill is looking further into it."

John nodded then stared out the window.

"Have you heard from my sister, Mags?"

Elvis shook his head. John had filled him in on Jen's difficult upbringing and her non-relationship with her sister.

"I'm afraid not, Max might know. I still can't believe he punched the professor in the face," Elvis chortled. "I heard about that guy and his draconian methods of construction."

Jen pursed her lips. John fired the Professor as soon as he heard of his lackadaisical attitude towards safety. Jen had made no objection.

Max walked in, nodded in their direction, then headed to the bar. He returned a few minutes later with a beer and some crisps. "So, what are we talking about?"

Jen smiled. "We're talking about a knight in shining armor who rescued my damsel sister in distress."

Max stood there, his face and neck flushing with embarrassment.

Jen and Elvis laughed. "At least some things don't change." Jen grinned even wider; she had heard on the grapevine that Mags had given Max a passionate kiss for his judicious motivational talk with the Professor.

Max gulped his beer and sat down. "Now that we have the Gnoll, what's the next step?"

Jen and Elvis shrugged as they all turned towards John expecting some brilliant plan. John hadn't heard any of their discussion. Suddenly his demeanor changed. The others around the coffee table could tell John had an idea.

Epilogue

Bridge, Gnoll Frigate *Wild Roar*

"Tempi Shipyards," Lord Saga commanded as she entered the bridge. The helm jumped to obey, twisting the attitude controller as the vessel headed out of orbit. Saga had transmitted her report from low orbit to her father while technically complying with his decree of banishment. He had reluctantly agreed to upgrade her ship. The shipyards were on the far side of the Gnoll Home system.

Saga paced on her bridge taking side glances of her crew for any signs of antipathy given they were exiled just as much as she was. Nothing. Saga took a deep breath relieved she hadn't had to face a mutiny and headed for her cabin.

Once she was alone, she dragged out a toy claw her brother had given her pretending it was the paw of a great Ancient Lizard kill he'd worn on occasions. "I stand alone now little brother. Betrayed by my family, my species, and the King. Revenge is such a small, petty word." Saga's jaws ached to bite hard. "I shall hunt down the creatures from that yellow ship and kill them all... *retribution* is a much better word."

Interrogation Room1, Rams Head Station

Mags quietly entered the room from behind the Ferret prisoner. He was standing in front of his chair, snarling at the marine on guard duty in the corner, who totally ignored the little hairball, which made the Ferret twice as angry. Suddenly from behind, Mags pulled the scarred Ferret down so hard he fell into his seat, stunned. The armed marine at the door turned toward the action but did nothing.

"You were trying to make a deal for the life of the Commander," Mags accused.

Glom twisted his head sideways to catch a glimpse of his interrogator. The permanent snarl slipped from his face when he saw Mags dressed as a Goth with piercings in her nose, tongue and five through her ears and eyebrow. Glom had seen species self-mutilate, but this was something more.

The spiky purple hair, black leathers and angelic white skin set her green eyes ablaze. "You should have made a deal for your own life." Glom opened his mouth to protest. "No, talking!" Mags snapped her fingers.

Glom's spoke, but nothing came out. His eyes widened at the silence. He yelled and could feel his throat vibrate, yet there was nothing but silence. With a remote in her pocket, Mags had turned on the noise canceling system used by security as a form of solitary confinement. It was a mild form of sensory deprivation used in prison as a punishment.

Glom tried yelling, his neck and head fur hackled as his mouth rapidly formed silent words. The device picked up his voice and, within milliseconds, broadcast through hidden speakers sounds that perfectly matched his voice with an inverse audio frequency. Just like noise-canceling headphones but better. Glom shook his head and tried again. Nothing. All sound was canceled.

Mags watched for Glom's voice cues as she turned the device off.

"You tried to sell my sister." Once again Mags turned the canceling device on.

Glom stared at Mags. Then started to protest, but naught came out of his mouth. Freaked, the Ferret cast his head about the room, looking for an escape. There was none.

"I should kill you now," Mags said calmly with a click of her fingers.

Glom's eyes widened, his tail fur stood on end.

"You would like that wouldn't you?"

Glom sat confused staring at the pale nightmare before him.

Mags continued, "Me to end your pathetic, miserable life; to end your suffering now because I can guarantee you won't recognize it by the time I'm finished with it... Speak," she clicked her fingers.

"Nooo-," he yelled. Glom was shocked he could now speak. Mags clicked her fingers and Glom was silent again. His eyes screamed with fear.

"Tell me about the Gnoll," she said.

Max's Station

Rezulin flicked his tongue to sample the air. Humans were smelly people despite the lengths they went to, to recycle the air through a conditioner. He could taste the floral hints from the perfume Commander Gale wore. It was fused with pheromones of adrenalin and sweat associated with anger. Ahh, her sister's scent was also present. Rezulin knew of the sibling rivalry.

The lizard turned back towards the console. The humans had given him access to their computers. He was staggered at how advanced they were. He now understood why humans had progressed so far so fast.

Rezulin thought of Darvus, the religious nut with something to prove for the old faith. Although Rezulin wasn't part of the Eki movement, Darvus' machinations made him think about joining. The crusty old lizard was the old guard. Rezulin smiled at the thought of not cleansing, it would really *get up Darvus' nostrils*. Humans had such interesting expressions. Rezulin switched screens searching for a comm to connect with S'sank. Maybe he knew the Ekis and who to contact.

Squishy Isle

"I cannot believe the Humans are following your advice," said Drakmok as his body turned green::Curious::.

"Which advice?" Tela said innocently.

"Hurrrumph. The *'pick a fight'* advice."

Drakmok pointed at Telas' chest with his third tentacle. His second one had been sliced off when a poisonous sea snake mistook it for its mate and tried to inject him with a paralyzing agent so it could impregnate him with eggs.

"You know the humans can't win against the Gnoll, let alone the lizards. Why give them false hope?"

Drakmok didn't see the hopeful smile in Tela's eyes. *They might just surprise you,* she said under her breath. "They need to learn to survive."

Drakmok's mantel flashed orange::anger::. "We have it good here, and you want to play games with the Humans?"

Tela sighed. "Nowhere is safe. I have given the Humans purpose."

Purple::mind shrug, no understanding:: infused Drakmok's tentacles. "Let's hope the Humans understand when they see your games for what they are."

Tela turned away, she didn't want Drakmok to see the Brown::fear:: and yellow::shame:: colors suffused her face. Many humans will probably die, and yet, she was sure she did the right thing.

The End

Acknowledgments

I wish to thank my family and friends who have spent hours reading and re-reading my scribbles.

Big thanks to Celia for her editing and keeping me focused.

There are places you can find me:

https://akbrown.info/

http://akbrownwriter.com/

http://squidpublishing.com/

https://www.facebook.com/AKBrownAuthor/

Please take a moment to leave a Review

Reviews on Amazon and Goodreads are vitally important to indie authors like me.

Amazon won't help market the books until they reach a certain level of reviews. So please, take a few seconds to click the stars and type a few words on how you liked the book.

Other titles by A.K. Brown

Champagne Universe Series

JumpStart Book 1

Humans on the Menu Book 2

Alien Invasion Book 3

Burning Stars Book 4

About A.K. Brown a.k.a. Tony Brown

Tony Brown has survived a spinal injury to become a quadriplegic at aged 16. He's been a Uni student, a Tax Auditor, a Child Support Officer, a Trainer, a Computer Analyst and is now a Self-Published Writer.

He has traveled from the artesian street markets of Paris' Montmartre to climb Samoa's lush jungles of Mt Vaea to see Robert Louis Stevenson's tomb. He's rafted from Guilin down the Li River in China's Guangxi Zhuang region and spoken to an assembly of kids at the local school on mischief in a wheelchair.

Tony now lives in a small house nestled between the leafy northern suburbs of Sydney where he writes science fiction and tip books for the disabled.

His debut Champagne Universe Series of books are a comic mixture of brain-sucking aliens, space battles and troubled morally devoid geniuses. Tony's long stays in the hospital provided him time and a real impetus to create rich and lively fantasy worlds to escape into.

One of Tony's favorite quotes from Dr. Seuss:

"You have brains in your head you have feet in your shoes. You can steer yourself any direction you choose."
Dr. Seuss, Oh, The Places You'll Go!

www.ingramcontent.com/pod-product-compliance
Lightning Source LLC
Chambersburg PA
CBHW051326250626
47155CB00007B/2475